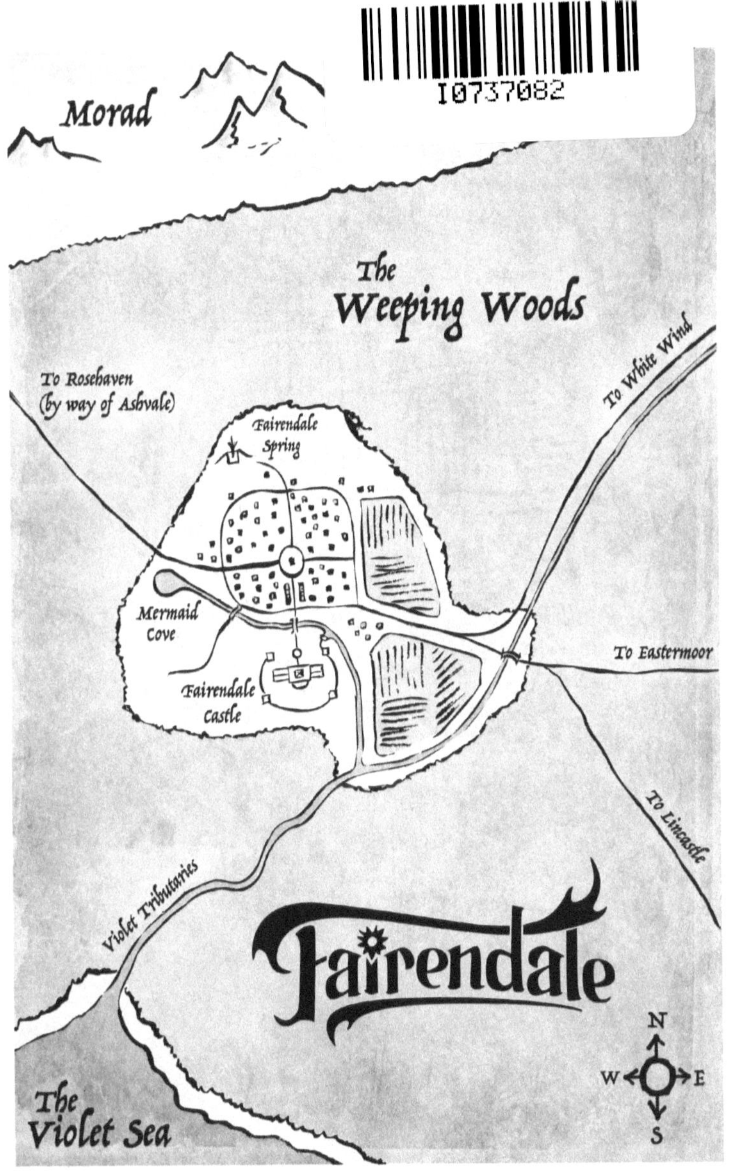

Morad
The Weeping Woods
To Rosehaven
(by way of Ashvale)
To White Wind
Fairendale Spring
Mermaid Cove
To Eastermoor
Fairendale Castle
To Lincastle
Violet Tributaries
Fairendale
The Violet Sea
N
W
E
S

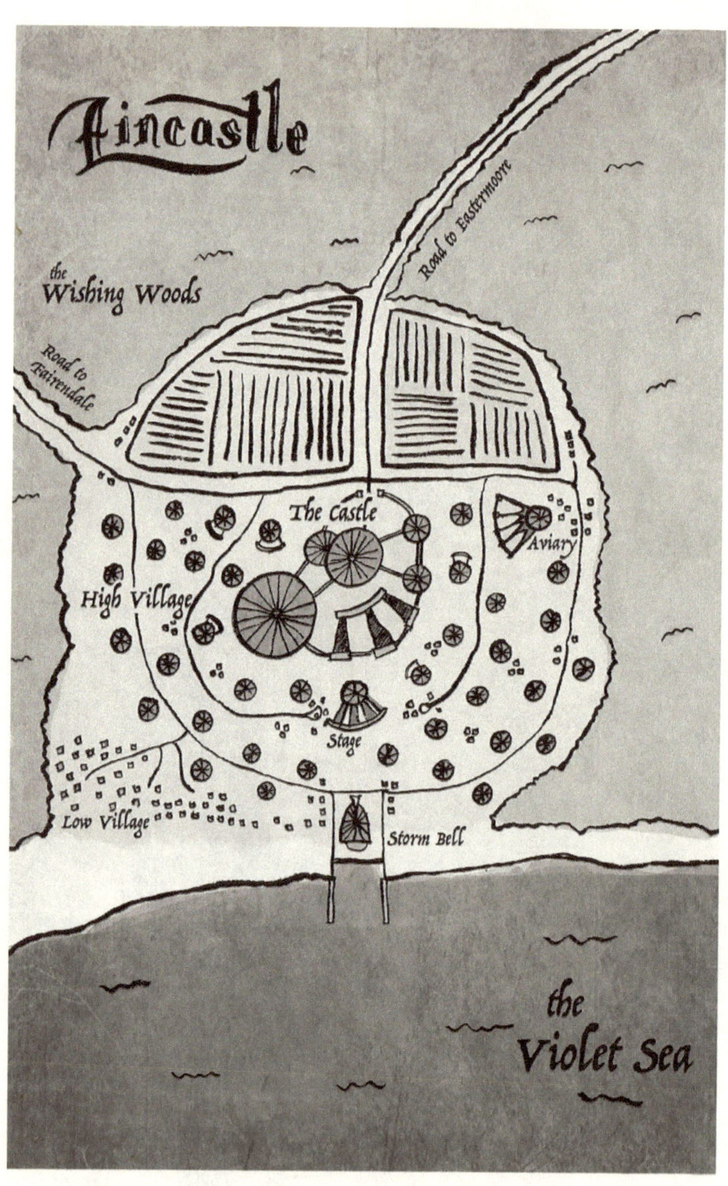

Fincastle
Road to Eastermoore
the Wishing Woods
Road to Fairendale
The Castle
Aviary
High Village
Stage
Low Village
Storm Bell
the Violet Sea

Fairendale

12

THE
BOY WHO LOVED
A SWAN

Read all the books in the Fairendale series!

Book .5: *The Good King's Fall (a prequel novella)*
Book 1: *The Treacherous Secret*
Book 2: *The King's Pursuit*
Book 3: *The Perilous Crossing*
Book 4: *The Dragons of Morad*
Book 5: *The Fiery Aftermath*
Book 6: *The Mysterious Separation*
Book 7: *The Boy Who Spun Gold*
Book 8: *The Boy Who Robbed the Rich*
Book 9: *The Girl Who Awakened the Beast*
Book 10: *The Boy Who Became the Wolf*
Book 11: *The Girl Who Built the Tower*

Collector's Editions:

Books 1-6: *The Flight of the Magical Children*

To see all the books L.R. Patton has written, please click or visit the link below:

www.lrpatton.com/writing

L.R. PATTON

THE BOY WHO LOVED A SWAN

BATLEE PRESS

Batlee Press
PO Box 591596
San Antonio, TX 78259

Copyright ©2018 by L.R. Patton
All rights reserved.
No part of this book may be reproduced or transmitted in any form or by any means, electronic or mechanical, including photocopying and recording, or by any information storage and retrieval system, without permission in writing from the publisher. For information regarding permission, write to Batlee Press, PO Box 591596, San Antonio, TX 78259.

The author appreciates your taking the time to read her work. Please consider leaving a review wherever you bought it and telling your friends how much you enjoyed it. Both of those help get the book into the hands of new readers, which is incredibly important for authors. Thank you for your support.
www.lrpatton.com

This is a work of fiction. Names, characters, places and incidents are either the product of the author's imagination or are used fictitiously, and any resemblance to actual persons, living or dead, business establishments, events or locales is entirely coincidental.

Printed in the United States of America

First Edition—2018/Cover designed by Toalson Marketing
www.toalsonmarketing.com

To A.R.T.
You are born to fly—
use your wings well

Return

The sun rises in the land of Fairendale, but it rises slightly to the northeast, as though it has forgotten the direction from which it is supposed to rise. It casts the land in a tip-tilted kind of light. Its people would say that at least the sun has risen today, for it has been many days since they have seen its golden glow and felt its warmth on their faces. But a sun that has forgotten where it is supposed to rise is more dangerous than a sun that does not rise at all, as the people shall soon understand. Its balance is askew.

King Willis, who is once more seated on Fairendale's gleaming throne, does not notice that the sun has risen at all. He stares straight ahead, as though awaiting further instruction. It is precisely what he is doing, dear reader, for something quite mysterious and unknown has overtaken him. A possession of sorts. If one could see inside the cells and bones and sinews of a person, one might see a green-tinted goodness gathered inside a recess of King Willis's mind, where the real King Willis is balled up and shivering while he sleeps, in miniature form. I know it is hard to understand. How could the real King Willis reside in the mind's corner of the man who sits on the throne? Well, it is simply the way of magic. He is there, and that is all you need to know.

But who sits on Fairendale's throne? That is not so easy to answer. It is King Willis, but it is not King Willis. It is a shell of King Willis, possessed by the cunning mind and nefarious spirit of another. It is unclear who, but if you have made it this far in the Fairendale chronicles (and if you have not, well, I suggest you begin from the beginning), we might make our guesses.

This shell of King Willis will think and plan and move, but you must remember that it is not the *real* King Willis who thinks and plans and moves. This may help ease your heart a bit, for what this king may do in the future—perhaps near, perhaps far—is something even I do not want to know yet.

King Willis stands and crosses the platform to the mirror. Its golden flourishes gleam in the sunlight that reaches through an open window and flings a blinding beam into the king's eye. He does not notice this, either. He stares, unblinkingly, into the mirror. He offers the looking glass a smile, one that turns up more on the right side than the left, but only slightly. An eyebrow arches.

"Mirror, mirror, on the wall," he says, and the mirror flashes to life. In the reflection, King Sebastien folds his hands across his fit middle.

"Where we go the world will fall," King Sebastien says, and the two men laugh, a sound that is hollow and wicked and alarming for those who may be listening. And in a castle like this one, there is always someone listening. Today, there are two—one at the back entrance of the throne room and another at the front.

"I must warn you, my son," King Sebastien says. He bounces on his toes and then places his heels back on the ground—though, in the mirror, there is no ground. He appears to float, stepping on nothing as he takes two steps forward. "You must not dine with the queen. You must not talk to the queen. You must not let her convince you that a king does not need a throne. She is a lovely woman, as she always was. And lovely women can never be trusted." His voice grows hard and sharp and shadowed at the edges.

"I will remain in here," King Willis says. "I will dine in here, I will sleep in here, and I will rise in here."

"Very well," King Sebastien says. "And I shall keep watch. As long as you do not dismiss me, I can remain."

"Yes, Father," King Willis says.

"And we will restore this throne to what it was always supposed to be."

"Yes, Father," King Willis says.

"We will make Fairendale strong again."

"Yes, Father."

"We will make its people suffer."

"Yes, Father."

"We will do what must be done."

"Yes, Father."

"You must not trust the queen."

"I will not, Father."

There is no hesitation, no weighing of consequences, no thoughtful consideration. There is only blind obedience. King Willis asks no questions; no questions even arise in his mind. It is, by his compromised logic, quite simple: King Sebastien is the rightful ruler. He will surely make the right decisions. He will make Fairendale great again.

"We have much work to do, my son," King Sebastien says. "We will restore this throne to its former glory. We will make it shine with brilliance." He pauses. "Are you ready?"

"I am ready, Father," King Willis says.

"Then we shall begin," King Sebastien says, and a flash of light, the sun catching on the mirror once more before it rises too high in the sky to reach through open windows, punctuates the words.

If you are as observant as I believe all of my readers are, you will notice several things about this exchange between King Willis and King Sebastien. You will first notice that there is no mention of the king of Guardia, King Wolfe, and his threat of invasion, which came in the form of a letter several days past. This is because King Sebastien does not worry over him at all. Even trapped in a mirror, he believes he is stronger than a king of giants.

There is also no mention of the imprisoned children, who remain in the darkest of all known worlds: the dungeons beneath the dungeons of Fairendale castle. This is because King Sebastien does not view children as people, only means to an end.

And, lastly, there is no mention of Prince Virgil, the heir to the throne, because King Sebastien, long ago, forgot what it means to love. He does not even know his grandson's name.

It is as though another story entirely is being written by the two men who meet in a mirror, a story devoid of all negotiation, compassion and, most tragic of all, love.

Calvin is in the Fairendale castle kitchen, doing a bit of light cooking—light cooking because day by day by day the castle's store of food diminishes. Garth, the king's page, is with him, for the king is occupied in his throne room, sitting on the golden seat, staring into space, or at least that was what the king was doing last time Garth peered through the gap in the rear door of the throne room. The two boys talk about the mice Calvin found in the dungeons beneath the dungeons on his last visit— mice that talk and walk on two feet and carry wooden walking sticks and wear dark spectacles. Garth is incredulous, and Calvin promises to bring him along next time he visits the children.

Their conversation shifts to the dire state of the castle. Food, for the first time in the history of Fairendale castle, has grown scarce.

"I do not know how Cook managed to keep the root cellar full," Calvin says. "I cannot manage to grow anything in the garden."

"But you took some vegetables to the children, did you not?" Garth says.

"A few," Calvin says. "There should be many more."

"You are doing as well as anyone can expect," Garth says.

Calvin throws a handful of old carrot pieces he found on the floor into a pot of water that boils on the cast iron stove. The boys watch it bubble, Garth pretending he did not notice from where the carrots came, Calvin hoping the boiling water will sanitize them.

"There is a blackbird," Garth says. "Out by the garden."

"A blackbird?" Calvin says.

"Yes," Garth says. "It has been gathering food in a basket." Garth stares at the floor, thinking. "There was a blackbird once," he continues. "It was said to have killed the king of Fairendale."

"I know the story," Calvin says, and he does. He has, on occasion, slipped through the castle library doors and taken a book or two back to his chambers. He remembers his mother and father reading to him as a boy, and sometimes the stories he reads himself help him feel less alone. Sometimes stacking books on the table beside his bed reminds him of his home in Ashvale, before it was swallowed by the eruption of a Fire Mountain, along with his parents.

"My mother lives in the village," Garth says. "She

sends me letters by pigeon." Calvin does not know what this has to do with a blackbird, so he lets his attention wander until Garth says, "My mother says that every morning the village people wake to a fresh supply of vegetables."

They are both quiet for some minutes, piecing together this new information. Does a fresh supply of vegetables delivered every morning mean that one of the village people sends a blackbird every eve to gather what the castle gardens produce? And is this such a terrible thing? They have, after all, lost their children. Is it not within their rights to pilfer from the castle when they have given so much, even if it was given unwillingly? Calvin considers this for a small amount of time, but his thoughts return, as they always do, to the immediate future and the imminent danger of starvation for not only those in the castle and the dungeons but all those in the village, too, if they secure their nourishment from his meager garden.

The kingdom grows grayer every day. Vegetables cannot grow without light. So perhaps it is not entirely his fault. But he feels as though it is. So many will die without food—food he was supposed to grow.

The sun is shining today. But it is only a matter of time before it disappears behind the gathering clouds in the sky.

Calvin turns away to stare into the fire. "I wish Cook were here," he says. He is still cross with Cook for leaving him.

Garth lets out a cry. Calvin twists his head to look at him. "What is it?" Calvin says.

Garth points. Calvin follows his long, bony finger to the window. He is not quite as tall as Garth, however, so he must stand to see what Garth sees. And when he sees it, when he sees *her*, his knees nearly buckle beneath him.

A strange sight emerges from the Weeping Woods. For a moment, Calvin believes that his mind has conjured the figure in his desperation to see it again, but then he looks at Garth. Garth's mouth hangs open. His finger still points to the window. He must see it, too.

It is the figure of a woman, cloaked in brown, stepping from the trees. The woman, he believes, must be Cook. Her face, obscured by a hood, lifts to the sky as if searching for the wind, and he sees that it is, indeed, Cook. The feathers of hope in his heart coalesce into strong, stable wings.

He has missed her so.

She is as large as he remembers—though it is not her thickness but her height that requires such a word as large. She is taller than any woman he has ever seen, and though she diminishes slightly as she walks from the trees to the path that leads to the castle, she is still an impressive and much welcome sight.

Calvin cannot speak. He cannot move. He cannot breathe.

As Cook moves toward the castle gardens, her old brown dress flutters around her ankles like a cloud of butterflies on the breeze. She looks this way and that, and as she searches the gardens and the lawn and the length of the castle, the expression on her face changes to one of sorrow.

Sorrow. When has Cook ever been sorrowful? Calvin marvels. He has only known a Cook who was sour and strict. Never sorrowful. Could it be that she loves this castle and its people? Could it be that she grieves its state? Could it be that she knows?

The shame warms Calvin's face.

Cook makes her way through the castle gardens, touching a sagging plant here, lifting the wilt of another there. The plants awaken around her, as though summoned by a long-awaited voice. It is astonishing to watch.

Magic. Does Cook possess the gift of magic? Calvin's heart thumps at the possibility.

Cook heads for the back entrance to the kitchen,

which looks out on the gardens. She momentarily disappears. Calvin keeps his eyes fixed on the door, waiting for the woman he has missed so very much, the woman he had grown to consider a mother of sorts. He waits for her to walk back through the door as she had walked out of it. Garth's fingers cut into his shoulder. He looks at Garth. Garth looks back at him, his eyes wide.

"You wished," he whispers. "And she came."

"It is only a coincidence," Calvin says. But his heart skips one beat and then another.

They have no time to say anything more, however, for the doorknob begins to turn ever so slowly. Garth and Calvin lean forward. The knob rattles, scrapes, screeches, but the door does not yet open. Garth and Calvin lean so far forward in the anticipation of the moment that Calvin loses his balance at the exact time the door swings open.

And there is Cook. Brown dress, brown cape, brown eyes fixed on him.

Calvin falls into her arms and does not feel the slightest bit ashamed when he begins to weep.

Cook is nearly barreled over by the boy. She did not

mean to stay gone so long, and she can see that her absence has had a profound effect on him. He has, if possible, grown even thinner. He has certainly grown more desperate. Her heart softens for a moment. Despite what he may believe about her, Cook is a woman of great love and adoration. And though she would not admit this to anyone within or without the castle, she has grown to love and adore this boy called Calvin.

So she permits him to stay for some time in her warm and welcoming arms. The other boy in the kitchen stares at her, but she allows her eyes to move to the iron stove, to the wash basin, to the mess strewn on the floor. When she is sure that Calvin has regained control over his relief, she pushes him away—gently, of course. She does not want him to feel unloved, but she also needs him to be strong. They will need strength for what is coming. And it is a precarious balance between cultivating love and cultivating strength.

Cook has never had a child. She does not know how to master this precarious balance, and she undoubtedly does not know what to do in this moment. So she does what she has always done, which is order and act.

"Tend to the fire," Cook says. "It must be stronger than that to cook what I have in mind." She meticulously shapes her voice into a bark so as not to seem too soft.

Calvin stares at her for a moment. "Well, go on, then," she says, adding a sprinkle of annoyance to the words. Calvin bolts. The other boy moves to help.

Good. More help in the kitchen. Perhaps the older one will be more competent than Calvin. But just as these words wriggle through her mind, the older boy trips, sending firewood in every direction. One of the pieces lands half in and half out of the iron oven. This would not be such a problem, except that the half-out piece touches her cutting table, and the fire dances toward the table's legs.

Cook rushes to the bit of wood and kicks it solidly into the fire.

"Sorry," the boy says.

"Perhaps you should look in on the king, Garth," Calvin says. His eyes move to Cook and then flick back to Garth.

"Very well," Garth says. He offers a slight bow and turns to go. But in the doorway, he spins on his heel. "It is good to have you back."

Cook watches him go and turns her attention to Calvin. "I will need some vegetables, whatever you can find," she says.

He shakes his head. "There are none," he says. "I have not been able to keep the castle gardens producing much beyond what I have already gathered today." He gestures toward the boiling pot.

"I think that you will find there are plenty," Cook says. "You have done well in my absence."

The boy stares at her for a moment. His eyes look as though they might swallow his face. She holds out a large basket. "Go on, then," she says. "Gather what you can."

He moves woodenly toward the door, looking back at her several times, as though to make sure she is real. She feels a hollow ache in her chest. She should not have left him for so long. She knew the cost.

When he is out the door, Cook surveys the dirty kitchen. She holds her cloak in one hand and touches the filthy surfaces with another. The kitchen is perfectly clean in moments.

Now, then. She must assess the condition of her Protection spell, which binds the walls and halls and dungeons of Fairendale from dangerous creatures. But first, a bit of nourishment. Everything is made better with some hot soup. She stirs the pot Calvin started. It fills of its own accord. She smiles. She sniffs. She turns.

Brownies. She can smell them. They must have slipped through the cracks of her magic while she was gone, and though they are not dangerous creatures, they are troublesome. And small creatures inside Fairendale castle means larger creatures are not far behind. She returned just in time. Tonight, she will revisit the brass knocker on the oaken entrance to the castle and bind this stone structure in safety once more. The creatures will not visit while she lives within the walls of the castle, for creatures are always afraid of shape shifters. But she has no way of knowing when she will be summoned next.

Cook turns back to the pot on the fire and stirs, thinking. She sniffs again. A smell has wandered in—earth mixed with a slight animal aroma. She turns. The boy has returned, and he is staring at her. The basket he carries is overflowing with vegetables.

"How?" he says.

Cook does not answer but, instead, gestures toward the wash basin. "Draw some water and wash them," she says. "We shall store them in the root cellar."

But the boy does not move. She sighs. "Go on," she says, and she is not talking about washing the vegetables.

"Where have you been?" he says.

"That does not concern you," Cook says.

"But you left us," he says. "You left me. You did not even tell me you would be back. I thought…" He does not finish.

Cook allows herself to step into the ache in her chest. She allows herself to look around at its rough and imposing walls. She allows herself a moment to recover. "I am back now," she says.

"And you will remain?" Calvin says.

Cook does not answer.

"You will leave me again?" Calvin says. "For good this time?"

Cook sighs. She rubs a hand over her mouth and chin, then lets it drop. "I had to see about something," she says. "I might have to do it again. But I will never leave for good."

"How do I know?" Calvin says. "How do I know you will not leave for good?" His glassy eyes cloud with a memory. "How do I know?" It is barely a whisper.

Cook turns so he will not see that she, too, is momentarily overcome. She cannot assure him of anything. She cannot promise him that she will always remain with him. She has a place in the realm, a purpose. And one day…

Well, one day she may not be human at all. The longer a shape shifter spends in his or her animal form, the more magic it requires to become human once more. This very afternoon, Cook stood for a long time on the perimeter of the Weeping Woods, trying to become Cook again, rather than a mid-sized bear. And she will have to become a bear again, much too soon. She can feel it.

Cook turns when the wash basin thumps against the kitchen wall. Calvin rolls it out the door and down to the well, to fill it with water. Cook is glad for the moment alone. She watches the boy from her window. She promises herself that she will not leave before he knows what she has been given to do. Perhaps it will make it easier for him to choose courage in the face of what comes if he knows what he must fear.

The boy returns noisily, dragging the basin behind him and sloshing it up the steps. Cook does not berate him as she might have done before. He begins to wash the vegetables and separate them into another large basket. Cook watches him for a moment. He catches her eye. "It is only me and Garth here," he says. "We are the only servants in the castle."

Cook's heart roars in her ears. "Only the two of you?" she says.

"Yes," Calvin says.

"What of Queen Clarion's maidservant?" Cook says.

"She left with all the others," Calvin says.

"And why did they leave?" Cook says. She studies the boy. His eyes are the color of golden honey.

"Dragons," Calvin says. "And the king has no more soldiers."

Cook clears her throat. "And why did you remain?"

she says.

Calvin looks at her for a long moment. "I had nowhere else to go," he says, and the moment curves around them, prolonged by words left unsaid. Calvin speaks into the chasm. "And I hoped you would return."

"Well," Cook says. She rubs her hands on the apron she has tied around her waist. "I am here now. And we shall get this castle back to its former state."

She is rewarded with a large and shining smile.

Oscar, one of the lost children of Fairendale, has had quite enough of sitting around on the edge of the woods, in a shelter that is utterly inexplicable to him. It looks like nothing, though he knows it must have been something. It appears to be only a repository for dust and dirt, and he is weary of hiding inside it.

He is weary, too, of watching the rich and opulent people of Lincastle strut about the streets as though they have nothing in the world better to do, as though they are the only ones in the world who matter. The geography books did not speak of this side of Lincastle. They only told of the homes that look like miniature castles, the sand on which birds of all kinds roam, and the castle made primarily of glass, unlike any royal abode that has ever been seen in the world.

Oscar would like to tell the people of Lincastle that he matters. He is a boy, stuck in a dusty shelter, twiddling his thumbs to pass the time, hoping no one will find him and return him to the king who pursues not just the magical children of Fairendale but all the ordinary ones—like him—too.

Well, he is finished with that.

He has seen, upon venturing from his hiding place, the bookshop that lies on the edge of town closest to his shelter. It is serendipitous that he ended up in a shelter near a bookshop. He has always loved books. In fact, his mother is a bookseller in Fairendale.

This bookshop is quite spectacular—three floors at least. His mother's shop was not quite so extravagant. It had only one floor, but that one floor was crammed with all sorts of magical and entertaining texts. Oscar had read them all and had a daily, perhaps even hourly, habit (which his mother had called annoying) of begging her for more. His mother was not the least bit interested in the new books that scribes sent to her or brought to her in person. She was more interested in the ancient ones that needed restoration. These texts fascinated Oscar as well. His mother had kept them in a special room off the back of her shop, where Oscar was always permitted to go and remain for hours and hours at a time, provided he was careful with pages.

As soon as he sees his mother again, he will tell her about this bookshop in Lincastle. He will tell her, too, that she should not visit such a pretentious place, as she has wanted to do all her life. He will tell her that Lincastle is a place where the people turn up their noses at a boy, no matter how clean he is. (He knows this about the villagers because the first day he found himself in a dusty shelter, he emerged into the light of day as a large, walking dust cloud. He washed himself immediately in the Violet Sea, but this made no difference to Lincastle's finest. Most of the people along the beach simply stared at him, their mouths gaping wide. Only one of the children spoke to him. "You will be taken by a sea monster!" she had said. But he paid that no mind. He knew about the stories parents told their children to keep them out of danger. He has now bathed in the Violet Sea for many days and has yet to be taken by a sea monster.)

Oscar has observed the bookshop in Lincastle for many days. He has seen people go in and come back out, rarely ever carrying a book in their arms to indicate a purchase. They appear to enter so as to seem interested in books and nothing more, projecting, they hope, a scholarly and cerebral image. He knows the kind. He, however, is a boy who truly loves books. Information books, story books, geography books, magic books, it does not matter. He loves them all.

And he would like one to keep him company.

Only one. Well, one and then another once the first is returned. He will not steal. He will borrow.

He has planned his strategy for days. He will sneak into the shop while the bookseller is distracted by other customers—preferably more than one; his plan is this: he will climb the stone exterior to the top floor, slide through the window there, slip a book into his tunic, and escape back out the window. He has always been good at climbing.

This is the day.

Oscar rises from his cramped place on the ground inside the shelter. He leans to the left and then to the right, his body aching from the crumpled up sleeping he has been doing of late. He misses his mother, who used to read to him every night before bed, and he misses his bed. A lump forms in his throat, but he swallows it. He must remain focused on the task at hand. He cannot allow himself a single distraction.

Of course, in the days since he woke from a Vanishing spell that carried him from the Weeping

Woods of Fairendale all the way to these woods outside Lincastle, Oscar, like the other lost children of Fairendale, has often found his thoughts returning to the other children with whom he escaped. In days past, he has thought of Maude and Arthur. He has thought of his mother and father and his tiny little sister. He has tried not to think of his tiny little sister, however, for the last thing he saw as he fled the village on the day the king's men came to round up all the children, was his sister's slight body, trapped in an iron cage. Rather than return to her and attempt a valiant rescue, the sight of her imprisonment only made his feet run faster into the Weeping Woods and what safety he could find there.

This is why he needs a book—to take his mind off that awful choice.

Oscar clears his throat. He stands in the doorway of his shelter, looking out across the streets of the village. There are beggars gathered in alleys. He had seen the men dressed in green who came into the village and gave the beggars some money, men whose faces are now plastered on random trees inside the woods, under the banner "Wanted." He had thought them brave and justified. He had even considered joining them for a moment or two, those archers who stole from the rich and gave to the poor. But his cowardice had resurfaced in the imagined eyes of his sister, and he had merely watched them from afar, silently cheering them on. (He could not even cheer out loud. He was the very definition of a coward.) And then the merry men had disappeared without a trace. He had looked for them, briefly, but the woods, in spite of his skeptical approach to the stories told about them, frightened him. He did not do an efficient job of looking. Only a cursory glance or two.

The town has now returned to the way it was—rich ignoring the poor, as though the people do not care that the merry men ever stole from them and tried to teach them a different way of life. No, he cannot say it has returned to the way it was, for he has seen one or two of the rich faithfully giving a bit of their coin and food and drink to some of the poor. So perhaps what the merry men did was not in vain after all. A few hearts changed is well worth the time and effort, is it not? His mother had always told him it was.

Oscar shakes his head. Here is yet another reason he needs a book. He cannot seem to go more than a few moments without thinking of his mother or his sister or Maude or Arthur or the other lost children of Fairendale. How he misses them all. How he misses Fairendale. Books would allow him an opportunity to immerse himself in another world—one much better than this one. He takes a deep breath. A tall man in a bright blue tunic walks into the bookshop. Two girls dressed in pink dresses follow him. A woman dressed in black enters a few moments later.

Now is the time.

He hesitates briefly, a small cloud of guilt stretching across his vision. It is true that his family was poor in the village of Fairendale, but he was never poor enough to steal anything as he feels he must do now. Even food is a necessity that he cannot acquire without stealing; he steals from the taverns every evening. The tavern keepers throw out their food into a small hole rimmed with stone. They do it for the birds, and Oscar has now grown accustomed to eating next to the birds—some smaller than his hand, some larger than himself—though the first time he came face to face with a bird that was taller than he was, he nearly ran away. Hunger rooted him in place, however, and now, if a tavern keeper happens to look out his window after throwing out the day's food, he or she would not see anything out of the ordinary. Oscar knows how to flap his arms so they appear as wings, and no one is the wiser in the shadows of dusk.

He steals water from the village fountains, after the people have all locked themselves inside their homes and extinguished their candles.

And now he has graduated to stealing books. His mother would be disappointed, but what else can he do?

He clenches his fists and moves on resolved feet toward the town.

As he walks into the village, he feels a hole in the toe of his shoe, and this makes him even angrier. Of all the possibilities in the world that could have transformed him into someone better during a Vanishing spell, why did he have to turn out to be the same old boy?

Oscar is unaware of the complications that arise around this question. Tell me, if you would: In the case of a Vanishing spell, would you rather appear as yourself or as a wolf, like Jasper; an old, bent woman, like Anna and Ruby; a dwarf, like Homer? Which do you think would be better?

Oscar's stature has not changed in the slightest, either, which he discovered the first time he tried to reach one of the mysterious torches that light the village streets. They have some kind of magical quality about them. A switch controls their fire.

Oscar is, this evening, distracted momentarily by this mysterious phenomenon, as he is every evening. He watches the torches flick on, all the way down the street, and he shakes his head.

Perhaps he will find a book about this magic.

When he reaches the bookshop, he must pull himself up over the windowsill in order to see into the lower window. His legs dangle from the ground, and he feels a grumble in his throat. He could have at least grown a little in the transformation. Would that have been too much to ask?

The bookseller is talking to the man with two young ladies. Oscar begins to climb, his feet finding notches in the stones easily.

He reaches the top floor with the window he has studied for many days. It is small, hardly wide enough for him to wriggle through. He opens it slowly and carefully, hoping it will not squeal its displeasure as the windows in his mother's shop had always done. The window slides open without a sound. He pokes his head inside and can hear the muffled rise and fall of conversation on the lower floors. He drops silently to the wooden floor and looks around him. He is in a sort of attic. It is dustier than he might have expected, as though these books have not seen a customer—or a feather duster—in a very long time. He touches a book, and his heart swells with anticipation.

He has missed reading almost as much as he has missed his family.

Oscar takes his time moving around the attic. He

studies the books carefully, meticulously, hoping that one will present itself to him as an undeniable first choice. But there are many he would like to read in this room, many old storybooks that remind him of his mother's ancient texts. He touches them all in turn, wiping dust mites from their tops. He pulls one out, puts it back, pulls out another, puts it back, on and on around the room. When he has touched them all, he stands in the center of the room, closes his eyes, and moves. The first book he touches he pulls from the shelf and shoves beneath his tunic.

He is nearly to the window, which is still open, when he notices a boy standing mute on the stairs, staring at Oscar with his eyes and mouth wide.

Oscar puts his finger to his lips, but it is too late. The bookseller has ventured up as well.

"You, boy!" the bookseller cries. How is it that Oscar, in making his detailed plan, did not ever consider this possibility? He is frozen in place, as though held prisoner by the bookseller's words.

Why had he taken so long to choose a book? Well, he knows why. He has always been much too enamored, too charmed, too infatuated with books. His love is not, in the slightest bit, rational.

Oscar looks briefly at the boy again, then jumps

through the window, all the way down to the ground. He winces as his ankle twists and then rights. He stops for only a moment before he sprints away, a limp hitching his gait, back toward the safety and cover of the woods. He does not even turn back to see if the bookseller is chasing him, or if the bookseller has sent the boy in his stead. Oscar has a singular purpose, and that is to return to the musty shelter in which he has spent the last fortnight, with the book safely in his hands.

The book emboldens him. A book has many purposes, some of them tangible, some of them intangible. In this moment, Oscar finds one of the intangible purposes of books: Courage—enough courage to plummet him into the woods he knows are not only haunted, if the stories are to be trusted, but also full of dangerous creatures. The trees swallow him whole, and only when he is fully inside does he turn and look back. The boy's face is pressed against the upper window of the bookshop, staring out at him until it is jerked from its place by a violent and invisible hand.

The night air, then, is filled with the shouts of a man and the cries of a boy, and a cold guilt crawls over Oscar's neck and back and shoulders. He hangs his head. He had not intended anyone to get hurt on his behalf. He grips the book in his hands and pulls it tighter to his chest, turning back toward his shelter.

Next time, he will have to be more careful and much quicker.

Oscar sits on a bulky bag of some kind or another, opens the lovely book, breathes in its comforting smell, and, with all the light that is left in the day, reads.

He flies on the wings of a story.

Home

Gladys, her husband, Yerin, and their son, Sebastien, had a very happy home. Sebastien, a young boy of seven, was an amenable child, who did everything his parents asked of him. He would putter about the kitchen, handing Gladys whatever she needed before she could even think to ask. He would help her cook, he would sweep out the loose layer of dirt that always settled on the bare floor, he would laugh at the uselessness of sweeping a floor made entirely of dirt.

"What is the use, Mother?" he would say, his eyes twinkling. "It will only get dirty again."

"That is the charm of a dirt floor," Gladys would say, her mouth pulling into a smile. "So that you, my dear, will always have an important job to do."

"Sweep out the top layer of dirt," he would say, and

he would move the broom in extravagant swishes. "It is what I was made for."

"You were made for greater things than this," she would say, and she was always immediately rewarded with his contagious grin.

After doing his duty in the kitchen, the young Sebastien would race out the door to the shelter behind their cottage where his father altered the elaborate dresses and gowns for the women of Lincastle. Bright colors adorned the walls and interior of his small work house, for Yerin, upon receiving a new gown and a request for alterations, would hang the gown from the tops of the ceiling and along the walls. If one were to peer inside the shelter at dusk, one might feel quite a fright to see so many dresses hanging, swaying in the soft wind that crept through the glassless windows as though ghostly people were gathered inside, dancing. Sebastien loved walking through his father's work house, which was much smaller than the cottage where they all lived. He would touch the fine silks and run his hands along the golden seams at the edges. He always thought his mother would look very beautiful in any one of these dresses, and he wondered why, with all his father's talent, he had never made one for her.

Sometimes, when Sebastien was helping his father, he

used a bit of his magic to speed the work along. His father did not mind, though he always warned Sebastien that magic did not come freely but always demanded a price. Sebastien did not quite understand it. He only felt weary after his work in the shop, but magic never asked anything more.

After the day's tailoring work was done, Yerin would pull up a chair to his work table, open a brown book with golden flourishes weaving in and out of studded jewels, and teach his son the nuances of magic, though Sebastien had more formal lessons with the town healer and resident prophet, Iddo. Yerin was a kind and patient teacher, and Sebastien was a careful and studious student. They would finish as the sun was setting, and the smell of soup would beckon them toward the cottage door. They would walk together, Yerin's arm around his son, and Gladys would greet them at the door, bidding them to wash up and come to supper.

It was a poor home, but they were happy.

As Sebastien grew older, eight and nine and then ten, Gladys and Yerin noticed that he began to pay more attention to their home. He would clean up where he could. He would touch up crumbling walls with his magic. He would waste his gifts on a bit of extravagance. He cared very much what his friends thought about him and his home.

And as the boy neared eleven, Gladys noticed the longing in his eyes when he looked at the other homes of the boys and girls of Lincastle. He began to notice that they looked like castles, while his home only looked like a hut. He began to feel a gap between who he was and who the other children were. He began to succumb to the spirit of Lincastle's heritage: greed.

This pained her to no end. It pained Yerin as well. Both of them had always been content with where they were in life, though Yerin still, occasionally, longed, with a searing sadness, for a life he had once been granted the opportunity to live in another land, only to have it ripped away from him with a single spell that saved his life. When he thought of this former life, he ran his hand along the puckered scar on his neck. He wore high collars so that others could not see it—not even his son. He did not want anyone to know that he had once been another man, had once been summoned back to life by a magic that had altered his face and his future.

Every day, Gladys and Yerin and Sebastien sat around the same table three times a day, to eat their meals and talk. Before every meal, Sebastien would grandly pull out his mother's chair, bow, and stand until she was properly seated. He called her a queen. He called his father a king and himself a prince. And at first, this was charming—endearing, even. But when it did not disappear as the boy grew older and wiser, Gladys and Yerin began to worry about their son. It was a niggling worry in the backs of their minds, but one day Gladys touched on it with a bit of teasing.

"I am no queen," she said, laughing. "Look at this dirty dress."

"But you should be," Sebastien said, and the darkness in his eyes grew darker.

"No," Gladys said, growing more serious now. "We do not need to be queens and kings to live a happy life. We already have one." She looked at Yerin and touched his hand. He smiled at her.

"I know," Sebastien said. But Yerin and Gladys both could see the glint in his eye, the longing. Royalty was what he wanted.

Gladys could not allow her son to fall into the trap of glory and power and fame, so she began to talk with him, the day after he turned eleven, about happiness and love and the demands of magic that were not always worth the risk. Perhaps she could sense that something was about to change. Perhaps that is why she told her son, "Your father loves you dearly, you know. He would do anything for you or me."

Sebastien nodded. His eyes softened, and she could see the love he held for his father shimmering in the brown. "I know, Mother," he said. "But I shall be able to do more. I know this."

"Perhaps," Gladys said. "But will it be worth what magic asks?" When the boy did not answer, she continued. "You have quite a gift for magic, just like your father did. I fear it will tempt you to do what you should not."

The boy's eyes lifted to hers, and he smiled so widely that her fears were put to rest in a single moment. "I will not do more than I should," he said, and she considered that a promise.

She never told him to use his gift of magic well and for good, for she always thought he would. She had no knowledge of his cruel and vicious future. Looking at her son, she could not even have imagined it. He was a good boy, a kind boy, a boy who spread love and laughter wherever he went. But eleven passed and twelve arrived, and the darkness in his eyes grew imperceptibly darker.

And perhaps, if Gladys had not at that time felt the sickness steal over her bones, she would have noticed, for a mother notices many things about her sons. Perhaps she might have addressed it.

But, as it happens, she did not have time.

One day, when Gladys stood beside the cast iron stove, stirring a pot of potato soup, she collapsed into a folded heap beside the warmth of the fire.

And this would change everything.

Decisions

It does not take them long to find Oscar. They come crashing through the door while he is sleeping. Six men. Six very large and bulky men. Six men who clamp their hands on him.

Last night he fell asleep with the book on his lap, and there it remains, so he does not even have a moment to hide it from their eyes and claim that they have found the wrong boy. When the men pull him roughly to his feet, the book clatters to the floor, and the sound of it is what heaves him more completely from the haze of sleep. He has not finished the book. He looks down at the leather cover and then up at the men.

"You are coming with us, boy," says the one in the front, his voice harsh and raspy. Oscar fights against them, as ferociously as he can, but of course his strength is nothing compared to that of six men. He sees the bookseller standing at the edge of the woods, a satisfied smile on his face.

The men drag Oscar to the town center, where he can see all the people dressed in all their wonderful clothes. The streets look like shining rainbows of red and orange and yellow and green and blue and violet. The people look as though they are the flowers of this land. His stomach twists. He misses the real flowers of Fairendale, the comforting scent of their sweetness. The streets of Lincastle smell of salt and sand.

A platform stands in the center of the village streets. On the platform stands a man with golden hair that shines like the hair of Oscar's sister and a face that looks much younger than should belong to a man. His blue eyes dance. "So," he says when the men thrust Oscar toward him. "We have another thief among us."

Oscar stumbles on his hands and knees in front of the man. The man grabs his hair and lifts up his head so that Oscar is looking directly in his eyes. "Tell me," the man says. "Do you work for the merry men?"

Oscar considers this. What if he says yes? Would it be more noble to stand on this stage and claim an alliance with the merry men? Would the merry men save him? Do they still exist out in the shadows of the woods? Are they watching now?

But, in the end, Oscar's cowardice wins yet again.

"No," he whispers.

"Speak up, boy!" the man says. "The people of the village cannot hear you."

"No!" Oscar says.

The man leans closer. "No, you do not work for the merry men?"

"No, I do not work for the merry men!" Oscar says. The people gathered round the platform let out a collective breath. Oscar meets the eyes of a few of them, who look almost immediately away. They are terrified of the merry men. Oscar does not understand this. If they are terrified of the merry men, then why have they reverted to their selfish ways?

The golden-haired man does not say anything for some time, which allows Oscar an opportunity to look around at the people. The dresses of the ladies sparkle in the sunlight. The tunics of the men are unblemished. The cheeks of the children glow with health. There is a girl, close to the platform, who is dressed more lavishly than the others. She wears a dress of blue shimmering silk, and a string of diamonds rings her neck. A pale blue hood hides her face. Oscar catches her eye, which is the same color as her dress—the kind of blue that resembles a Fairendale sky. His stomach twists again.

Such extravagance. They do not even know what they have. They look at him as though he is a vagabond, as though he is the least among them, but he has more than they have. He has compassion. Love. Conviction. He is glad he is who he is.

Let them kill him. He has no place left to go.

No. Do not let them kill him. He would like to see his mother and father and sister again someday.

In the silence that stretches between Oscar and the golden-haired man, Oscar is torn one way and then another. The golden-haired man finally speaks, settling Oscar on the words, *Do not let them kill.* "I am the law keeper of this land," the man says. "And you have stolen."

The people murmur. The law keeper holds up his hand. "Do we have a witness?" he says to the crowd.

"Aye," says a man's voice, and the crowd parts so that the bookseller can step forward. He points at Oscar. "This boy stole a book from my shop. One of the rare and valuable ones." The bookseller holds up the very book that Oscar fell asleep reading last eve. A piece of cloth, which he tore from the bottom of his tunic, flutters to the ground, effectively losing his place. Oscar balls his hands into fists.

The law keeper looks back at Oscar. "Well," he says. "And what have you to say to this accusation?"

"I only meant to borrow it," Oscar says.

The law keeper laughs. "You only meant to borrow it." The people laugh as well.

Oscar scowls.

"Tell me, boy," the law keeper says. "Out of all the things in this village that you could steal, why would you steal a book?"

Oscar does not even hesitate to answer. "A book is the most valuable of all treasures," he says. "Nothing compares to its worth."

The law keeper laughs again, and the people echo him. "You believe that a book is more valuable than a store of diamonds or a room full of gold or a fine dress?"

"Yes," Oscar says. He is unflinching.

The law keeper throws back his head and roars his laughter. "Well, I suppose that explains a few things," he says when he is finished. He pulls Oscar to his feet and then up off his feet so that his boots show more clearly to the throng of people. Oscar tries to hide the boot with the hole in it, but this is the one the law keeper would like on display for all these people gathered in the courtyard. The law keeper continues, with a barely hidden laugh wrapped securely in his words. "I suppose that explains why you did not steal boots."

Oscar's toe dangles out of the boot. He feels upon him the eyes of the girl in the pretty blue dress, and shame climbs his skin in a blaze of red.

The law keeper sets Oscar on his feet again, turning him to face the bookseller, who has crossed his arms across his broad chest and pulled his lips into a disagreeable frown. "What do you ask of the boy?" the law keeper says.

"Pay me what I am due," the bookseller says. "Plus interest. It is the way of things in Lincastle." He lifts his chin and stares at Oscar.

Oscar arranges his face into the steadiest gaze he can manage. "I do not have money," he says, and he, like the bookseller, lifts his chin. "It is why I borrowed the book."

The crowd gasps, as if a thief who has money is somehow better than a thief who has none.

"If you did not have money, then why did you enter my shop at all?" the bookseller says. His graying mustache twitches. His face has turned a dark shade of red, nearly violet.

"I love books," Oscar says, simply. "I have missed them."

The bookseller looks at him, his mouth agape. Then he shakes his head. He turns to the law keeper. "I demand that this boy be locked up so that he does not steal from any others in this village."

The people shout their agreement. Oscar's muscles tense. He will run. It is the only thing left to do.

"Should this boy be locked up, or should he die?" the law keeper asks the bookseller. But the people act as though he is asking them, and they begin to chant their answer.

"Die!" they say. And again. "Die!" Again and again and again. It becomes a chant. "Die, die, die!"

Oscar's knees falter. He feels as though he is in some kind of theatrical production, one performed to entertain the people. And understanding slowly breaks over him. He *is* an entertainment. He is an entertainment to people who must, at every turn, be entertained. It is all the merry men were, though they left a piece of fear in their stead.

And now he is angry. He clenches his fists. He stands to his full height. He shouts. "Your land is a terrible land. You do not know how to love. You do not know how to help. You do not know what it means to live as humans."

The people laugh, and then their shouts grow louder. "Die, die, die!" He turns this way and that, looking for some break in the crowd, some escape route he might be able to secure, some compassionate face he might be able to sway. There is only one.

He meets the eyes of the girl in blue. Hers are exceedingly sad, so sad that his own blur. She is only a girl. What could she do to help him?

And then she steps forward and lowers her hood. Her dark hair shines. "Unhand him," she says quietly. Oscar does not think she will be heard above the chanting of the people. But, remarkably, their cries fade, as though every one of them heard her speak. The whole world goes silent for a moment, and Oscar holds his breath.

"Princess," the bookseller says. "I did not know you were here among us."

"Because you were more concerned with your blood money," the girl says, and Oscar almost smiles. She delivers the words kindly enough, but they are fierce underneath the kindness. It is a gentle but public reprimand, and Oscar hopes it stings as viciously as he has been stung. The princess turns her attention to the law keeper. "Unhand him," she says again.

"But Princess Freya," the law keeper says. "This boy has stolen from the village."

"I shall pay for the book," Princess Freya says. She casts her eyes upon the bookseller for a moment. "Plus interest."

"That shall not be necessary," the bookseller says,

staring at the ground.

"Now," Princess Freya says. "Tell me, Captain Nottingham, will you unhand the boy, or shall I send for my father?"

A vein in Captain Nottingham's neck bulges, but he releases Oscar. "Very well, then," he says. "But if he steals again…"

"He shall have no need to steal again," Princess Freya says. "I shall make sure he has all he needs and desires." The princess moves swiftly forward, takes Oscar's arm, and leads him away from the crowd. Oscar can feel every eye fixed on him. He can think of nothing to say.

He expects her to tell him to be on his way and not to steal again when they are outside the view of the villagers, but her arm continues to thread through his, and she leads him toward an inn. At the inn, she gestures toward a table, where they sit together, where Oscar will eat his first hot meal in a very long time.

The princess lets him eat, and only when he is finished does she speak.

"From where do you come?" she says.

Oscar swallows hard and takes a drink of his water to stall. "Another land," he says at last. "My mother was a bookseller there."

The princess looks at him, waiting for him to say

more, but he does not.

"Why did you take the book when you needed much more?" she says.

Oscar shrugs. "My passion for books is not always logical," he says. "Or so my mother used to say."

Princess Freya laughs. "Logical," she says. "No, I suppose passions are never logical." She traces a wood pattern on the table.

"My mother's bookshop operated on a lending system," he says.

"And you thought this one did?" Princess Freya says. She lifts her eyes to his, and he is swallowed whole in their blue.

"No," he says. "I knew I must pay for the book. I did not have money."

"You must not steal again," Princess Freya says.

"But I do not have money," he says.

"The castle has much," Princess Freya says. "I meant it when I said I would supply what you need and desire."

Oscar is overcome by the generosity of this girl he has only just met. "But why?" he says.

Princess Freya looks at him for a long time, and then a smile breaks across her face, warming it like a golden sun gilding land in the early morning. "Because my passion for books is not always logical either," she says.

A warm feeling trickles into Oscar's chest, swells, and bubbles out into a laugh. Princess Freya joins him. They turn a few heads in the dining hall, but neither of them cares.

"I must be on my way," Princess Freya says, pushing back from the table. "But perhaps we can meet tomorrow, on the shore of the Violet Sea." She raises a thin brown eyebrow at him. "You are the boy who immersed himself in the Violet Sea, are you not?"

Oscar looks down at his feet. "Yes," he says. "I am."

"Brave or merely foolish?" she says, and her smile is contagious.

"Perhaps a little of both," Oscar says.

Princess Freya nods. "You will find all you need waiting for you inside your room," she says.

"My room?" Oscar says.

Princess Freya nods toward the innkeeper. "You only have to ask for your key, and you shall sleep warm and safe tonight."

Oscar's words lodge in his throat, but Princess Freya seems to understand what it is he needs to say. She pats his arm. "You will thank me with friendship," she says. She glances around the room, her eyes stopping nowhere. "It is quite lonely being a compassionate person in a village like this one." Her eyes lock back on Oscar. "I do what good I can. And I hope it is enough."

"Thank you," Oscar finally manages to say.

Princess Freya says nothing more, only turns and heads out the front door.

When Oscar arrives at a room that is larger even than the one he had in his Fairendale home, a new pair of boots, a clean change of clothes, and the book, his place held by a cloth that resembles Princess Freya's dress, is waiting for him.

Oscar smiles, tears tracing paths down his dusty cheeks.

It is good to be seen.

"Never Land sounds like it may be our only option," says a boy called Fineas. Deep in the Wishing Woods near Lincastle, there is a group of boys, lost children from Fairendale, gathered just outside a ramshackle shelter that leans more than slightly to the right. The boys were left here when Theo, another of the lost children of Fairendale and the magical boy for whom King Willis searches with such kingly persistence, returned to the kingdom so that he could surrender to the king and save the remaining children.

But the children are still on the run, Theo has not returned, and danger seems to press in on every side. August, the unspoken leader of this group of boys, fears that it is because Theo never made it back to Fairendale, for whatever reason. And there are many possible reasons. Perhaps he was mauled by monstrous creatures in the miles of forest that stretch between Lincastle and Fairendale. Perhaps he could not find food or water. Perhaps he is injured somewhere, calling for help even now.

All of these possibilities pinch the heart of August. So do the words Fineas has introduced. And so, especially, do the looks from the other boys, who appear to be considering this Never Land as a viable option for them all. A way out. A happy ending.

Nearly three days ago (or has it been four? The question gives August a burst of hope.), at dusk, a large group of fairies visited their small shelter and told the boys about a land where children never grow up. They would be fed, watered, cared for. They would have each other. Never Land sounds like a magical, utopian place, but August cannot shove away the doubts that rise within him—doubts that say not all about this land is as it seems.

The fairies gave them three days to make their

decision: do they want to go to Never Land, where they never have to grow up but can never return home, or do they want to remain in this cold and broken homeland?

He is sure it has been four days. Perhaps the fairies forgot.

August squares his shoulders. "We must remain here," he says, as he always does. He does not know anymore if it is out of loyalty to his best friend or simply habit.

"Because Theo told us to remain," Fineas says. He flings his hands out and then drops them back to his side. "Theo, who is not here."

"He will return," August says, but his voice is chipped.

"Do you see anything about this land changing?" Fineas says. "He has done nothing." The words ring out in the small clearing, bouncing against the trunks of trees so that it sounds like three other voices join the one. Fineas shakes his head. "What did Theo leave to do?"

August has avoided this question for some time. He has avoided many questions from the other boys, but he sees now, by the dark looks on their faces, that he cannot avoid them any longer. He sighs and speaks slowly. "Theo returned to Fairendale so that he could surrender himself to the king."

The other boys draw in heavy breaths. Even Fineas drops his mouth open.

"Theo had the gift of magic," August says. Though this is a secret that has slipped out several times, the boys have never discussed it. "The king was pursuing him."

"The king was pursuing all of us," Leo says. His dark eyes flash. "He would not stop at Theo."

August feels something shift in his chest, and a small bit of warmth climbs up to his throat. "I do not believe he would either," he says. "But I worry about Theo. I worry that he never made it back." His voice cracks open, spills out on the ground, and wavers there.

The boys are silent for a time.

"Then perhaps we should return to Fairendale," Fineas says. It surprises August, for he did not know that Fineas cared so much about Theo. He seemed determined to convince them they must go to Never Land instead.

"But what about Never Land?" says a boy called Henry.

Fineas looks up at the sky, which is a lovely blue. "We would not be able to return," he says.

"So you have your doubts as well," August says.

"Does not everyone have doubts about everything?" Fineas says. "How does one ever know what is right?"

August pats his chest. "My heart can often tell me," he says. "It is my mind that often leads me astray."

"Logic," Fineas says. "And love."

"They are a difficult balance," August says.

"And what does your heart say about this?" Fineas says. The other boys watch them, as though they are spectators in a theatrical production of some kind. August feels the sudden urge to laugh, but he does not.

He takes a moment to answer, and then he says, "My heart says to remain here. I love this land. I want to see it return to its former beauty and order."

"I do not think our current king will accomplish that," Fineas says. "His actions only tear it further apart."

"Then perhaps we need a new king," August says, and his eyes rise to meet the gray ones of Fineas. Fineas smiles slowly.

"Perhaps we do," he says.

"Then we are agreed?" August says. The other boys look from August to Fineas and back again.

"Agreed about what?" Ernest says.

"Theo is our king," Fineas says. "And Theo is the one we will see seated on the throne, even if we have to make it so."

August nods his head, and the rest of the boys begin to nod vigorously, too, as though they knew this all along and only needed someone to voice it for them. They stand up and whoop and holler and skip around like wild and unruly creatures. They are so taken by this new development, this novel and exciting plan, this hope of returning to their home, that they do not notice the long line of fairies assembling in front of their makeshift shelter, glowing in every color imaginable.

And before they can notice, their legs buckle, and they fall where they stood, in varying positions of sleep.

A fairy with golden hair pinned to the top of her head flutters her opaque green wings and folds her tiny hands across her miniature red gown. She lifts her head. She smiles.

"Foolish boys," she says. "We will haunt your dreams, then."

Arthur, former magic instructor for the children of Fairendale, and Zorag, the dragon king of Morad, stand on the edge of the woods that lie slightly south of the dragon land of Gyria, which is slightly to the north of the kingdom of Ashvale. The land of Gyria looks very much like the land of Ashvale: arid, forlorn, desolate.

Arthur shifts beside Zorag. "Are you sure there are

dragons in this land?" he says.

Zorag growls softly. "They know how to hide well," he says. "But they are here." After a moment, he continues: "I cannot hear their hearts, but I can smell them. A dragon can never hide his reptilian scent."

Arthur wrinkles his nose. The dragons here smell of smoke and sulfur and death—a thick, sour, choking scent. Travelers who braved the crossing of this land would likely attribute this smell to the Fire Mountains, but it is really the dragons, who are really the Fire Mountains. This is the information Zorag has given Arthur. In his earlier days, when Arthur traveled across all the lands of the realm, he crossed Ashvale—even came close to seeing the eruption of a Fire Mountain. He never would have guessed those Fire Mountains were dragons.

Are they really? Arthur shoves the question away.

From here, Arthur can see all across the land. There are many Fire Mountains, which means there are many dragons. The ground beneath them rumbles. Arthur clears his throat. "And we must visit these dragons next?" he says. He is, to tell the truth, somewhat frightened of dragons who breathe liquid fire.

A puff of smoke wheezes from Zorag's mouth. It curls into some words: "We are here." Arthur has come to know the dragon well during this journey, and he knows that Zorag, now, is mildly annoyed. Well, who can really blame Arthur for trying? These are dragons who breathe liquid fire.

"There is a hierarchy within the dragon lands," Zorag says, by way of explanation. "One cannot visit the next dragon land in the hierarchy until the ones before it have been visited."

"And this land is the next on the list," Arthur says.

"Precisely," Zorag says.

Arthur shivers. Fear heaves into the opening in his throat, making it hard to breathe. Ashvale used to be a thriving village. Many years ago, an eruption of the Fire Mountains—timed perfectly in a massive wave of red, according to the stories—wiped out all the people and their homes. The liquid fire cooled over the tops of bodies and wood and stone, leaving a ground of blackened rock. A handful of people tried to rebuild in Ashvale, but they, too, were consumed in another eruption eight years ago. No one has ever attempted another rebuild.

Thinking in this direction causes Arthur's fear to lengthen and stretch in his chest.

"Perhaps we should wait another day?" Arthur says.

"Evening is the best time," Zorag says. His words are short and clipped. He is even more annoyed at Arthur now. But Arthur does not care. No, it is not true that he does not care—he only cares for his safety more than the annoyance of the dragon.

"I thought you said that evening is the time when dragons believe any intruders on their land come in war, not peace," Arthur says, for this is what Zorag told him of the dragons of Eyre, the first dragon land to which they journeyed in hopes of mobilizing a dragon army. Instead, they found Zorag's dying uncle, received an apologetic dismissal, and were properly and thoroughly cast out of the land by an angry heir of the dragon king.

If that was the best reception they will get during their journey, Arthur feels like he might need a bit more preparation time.

But Zorag only growls. "Every dragon land has the same unspoken rules but different underlying ones," he says. "These dragons are unlike the others in every way they can be."

"Ah. Rebels."

Zorag does not say anything.

Arthur considers pointing out that perhaps the rules have changed in the years since Zorag has visited these dragons, but he does not want to risk shaking the dragon's courage. At least one of them should have a healthy dose of courage.

The dragon waddles forward onto the land. Arthur follows, every step both a pain and a terror.

Dragons, when on the ground, are not nearly as majestic as they are in flight. They are not accustomed to traveling long distances on their feet, and their tails become cumbersome and awkward, slinging out behind them and causing their long, sleek bodies to waddle significantly. They lumber rather than slither. They stomp rather than step. Their hind ends shake rather than glide. Arthur has grown accustomed to Zorag's awkward land gait, but it would likely amuse his son and daughter to watch it. This makes him smile. He hides it quickly so the dragon does not see.

Arthur was shocked to discover that there were more dragon lands than Morad, where Zorag is king. He had not been aware of this, perhaps because the dragons of other lands were never on friendly terms with villagers, and, for the most part, avoided them. There were stories, of course, as there are stories about every mysterious creature in the lands. The stories tell of dragons who guarded treasures, dragons who guarded magical trees, dragons who lived at the bottom of the sea and guarded the deep.

No stories tell of dragons who are Fire Mountains. He will have to tell these himself—if, that is, Zorag's claim is true. Arthur is somewhat ashamed to note that doubt lingers in his mind. So Arthur begins a silent story now, to take his mind off his uncharacteristic skepticism and the treacherous path that, at any moment, could shift into a large and looming dragon. They could be walking on a dragon. Arthur looks at his feet and then quickly back up.

A Fire Mountain in the far distance spits out red liquid into the sky. It glows and then falls in a spray of large and steaming drops. Arthur does not see where it lands.

"Take care where you step," Zorag says. They stand well within the bounds of the land now. Another Fire Mountain erupts in the distance, and the ground shakes beneath their feet. It appears that the Fire Mountains are warning them to go back. Flee.

Arthur very nearly does. He cannot do this.

But the dragon moves forward, so Arthur, his hand clutching the smallest part of the dragon's tail, does, too. After a time, he looks back. The woods seem very far away.

Zorag suddenly stops. His head tilts to the side.

"What is it?" Arthur says, his heart clattering in his chest.

"Quiet," Zorag says, and he listens, his head cocked.

In a moment, he lowers his head so it is even with Arthur's face, and he says, "Run."

Arthur runs.

He does not know why he runs, nor does he really want to know. He does not look back, does not turn to the right or the left, does not stop until he is safe—or as safe as he can expect to be—inside the woods again. The large and leafy trees surround him with a semblance of calm. He breathes. He waits.

The dragon crashes into the trees and then halts as abruptly as he entered. He pants, smoke escaping from his wide, round nostrils.

When it appears that the dragon has regained his breath, Arthur says, "What was it?"

"A creature," Zorag says. "A basilisk. Larger even than a dragon. But he does not appear to be able to cross the line of the land. He tried, and something held him back."

Arthur knows all about basilisks. Those large snake-like monsters with eyes that can turn you to stone and venom that can burn your skin worse than any fire. He shivers.

It is a reminder that there are more dangers than dragons here.

"I do not know why the dragons of Gyria would live

with a basilisk in their land, unless…" Zorag looks around him.

"Unless?" Arthur says.

"Unless this is the wrong entrance."

"But there are many entrances," Arthur says. "How would you know?"

Zorag does not say anything. After a time, the dragon ventures out of their small clearing, much to Arthur's horror, and when he returns after what seems, to Arthur, like an eternity, he says, "It appears that the basilisk is gone. We will pass the night in the land."

"In the land where a basilisk chased us out?" Arthur says. It seems quite foolish to him that they would risk their lives so recklessly.

Zorag's yellow eyes glow in the approaching darkness. "It is the only way," he says, and he moves back toward the land. Arthur stares at Zorag's retreating figure for a time, and then he follows the dragon, in spite of his dread.

They do not travel far into Gyria before Zorag says, "We will sleep here."

Arthur looks down at his feet, at the black rock beneath him. He looks behind him, at the lush green grass of the forest. One of them would clearly make a better resting place than the other. So he says, "Perhaps I can sleep in the forest, on a bed of grass."

"You must remain," Zorag says. "Or you will be in danger."

Arthur throws up his hands. "But there was a basilisk. Are we not in danger here, too?"

"We are in more danger if we sleep in the woods outside Gyria," Zorag says. "I have remembered another rule of these dragons: When a foreign dragon lies down and sleeps within the bounds of Gyria, it means that there is no enmity between the dragon clans. It means we do not come to fight." Zorag blinks his eyes at Arthur. "This is why we must remain here."

Arthur tilts his head and studies the dragon. "And you have only just remembered this rule," he says.

Zorag lift his head. "There are many rules to remember," he says. "It has been some time since I reviewed them."

Arthur bites his lip to keep from saying, *Well, perhaps you should review them before we venture into another dragon land.* After a time, he does what he is expected to do: He sits on the cold black stone and then lies down on it and then twists and turns, trying to find a spot that will not crumple his back into wrinkles by morning. It is a difficult thing to do.

"What about the basilisk?" Arthur says when the two

of them have lapsed into a long and heavy silence.

"It will not return," Zorag says.

Arthur props himself up on one elbow. "How do you know?" he says.

"Sleep," Zorag says. "I will keep watch."

Arthur sighs, but he drops again to his back, which will surely ache terribly by first light. He is so tired, however, that it does not take long for sleep to find him, roll him up, and tuck him in tight for the duration of the night.

This is why he does not even stir when Zorag slips a scaled arm beneath him, pulls him closer to his dragon body, and wraps him in warmth. This is why, when a vision flickers across the mind of the dragon—a vision of the young man who was his second rider—and the dragon shakes his enormous head to clear what cannot be, Arthur does not even feel the slight tremor in the dragon's body. This is why, when the dragon realizes that he is coming to love this man as he had once loved his rider and the dragon recklessly roars his pain, Arthur sleeps on.

The dragons of Gyria, however, do not.

Healer

It was quite unexpected, the way it all happened. There were no signs. Gladys was one day perfectly healthy and the next day a thousand years old, or so it felt. The day Gladys collapsed at the hearth of her stove, her son had been coming through the doors, sent on an errand to fetch a tool by his father. He saw his mother's dark hair lift and spread in mid-air, as her legs buckled beneath her. He watched in slow motion, rooted to the spot where he stood, as her knees hit the floor and her hair jerked and then her upper half slammed into the dirt. He screamed.

Yerin came running. He knelt beside Gladys and shouted something to Sebastien, but the boy did not hear it. When Yerin had gathered Gladys carefully in his arms, he said it again.

"Go fetch your teacher," Yerin said. The boy stared at him. "He is a Healer!" Yerin added, and the boy took off running.

Iddo was in the middle of work; he had, in the days after his wife's death and his son's mysterious disappearance, become quite obsessed with a particular work that was done in the dark and in secret. He heard the boy calling like a strange clenching in his heart (though later he would wonder how this could be) and quickly turned from the table and rushed out of doors, only for the simple fact that he did not want to be discovered. People in the town of Lincastle did not take well to experiments. But since he had given his powers of magic to a boy who was no longer in and of this world, all Iddo had left was science and experimentation.

They called him a Healer and a prophet. They did not know that he healed and prophesied with science, not magic.

His heart throbbed when he saw the boy before him. Sebastien was the same age his son, Jared, would have been this year, had he not disappeared—died, perhaps. Iddo was quite old. Jared had been born to him in old age, and he had loved him dearly. Now another boy, a darker one where his son had been fair, stood before him, and Iddo felt the sadness ripple through his chest.

"Yes, what is it?" he said. He could see that Sebastien was distraught. He taught the boy a bit of magic every day, and he knew him quite well.

"My mother," Sebastien said. "She is sick."

"I shall be there shortly," Iddo said. He knew where the boy lived and who his father was, for Yerin had sought him out to teach Sebastien magic when the boy had turned eight, back when Jared was learning the ways of magic, too. "Run along home." He watched Sebastien turn around and run as fast as his legs could possibly run. He stared after the boy for a time, and then he returned to his underground workshop and the body lashed to the table.

"I shall return to you, my dear," he said, and then he extinguished the torch and reached for his staff. It did not take him much time to reach the home of Yerin and Gladys. It was very near his, on the edge of the town. The poorest of Lincastle were relegated to the edges. The poor included prophets like himself and Yerin.

When Iddo entered the home, he came face to face with a man who looked so like his father as a younger man that he very nearly cried out. His father had disappeared five years ago, without a single note or hint of goodbye. Iddo had not spent much time looking for him, however, for Folen was not the sort of father one would spend time looking for. In fact, Iddo felt happier with Folen gone, for he could perform his science, which his father had always condemned, in peace.

But the man before him was not his father, and Iddo's breath soon returned to normal. He had not seen Yerin in some time. The man had grown significantly older. Sebastien tugged at Iddo's hand, and the prophet's heart twisted. He had loved a boy, a son, once, and the weight of it was nearly suffocating.

Sebastien pulled Iddo into a tiny bedroom with only a single bed and a small wooden chair at its side. Only a shuffling step behind him told him Yerin was following.

Upon entering the room, Iddo knew, by the shrunken air within it, that this sickness was much larger than his skills could eradicate. But still, he went through the motions, knelt at the side of the bed and touched the beautiful woman's face, which looked much too young for death, and her forehead and the hands that were cold at her sides. He had some herbs and poultices that might cleanse and sanitize and ease the pain of her suffering, but they would not save her. He turned to Sebastien and Yerin. Their eyes looked on him with such great hope that he could not tell them what he had to say. He only dropped his eyes and lifted his staff above the woman. He held it there, aloft, and closed his eyes, reciting the enchantments he had learned for show. Only this time, he hoped it was for more than mere show. He hoped he could save her. These people were good people. Death should not come for good people.

It was all a ruse. He did not feel the warmth he had felt once when he possessed the gifts of magic and healing. He had once been great, sought after as a man of significant achievements.

But his enchantments, his staff, would change nothing. He dropped his hands to his side. "I will fetch some herbs that may help her sleep," he said, leaving many other words, such as, *It will only ease her passing*, unspoken.

After many days and weeks of visiting Gladys and only a worsening of her condition, Sebastien shouted at Iddo as he walked in the door of the cottage. "Why is she not better?" the boy said. "Are you really a Healer?"

Iddo looked at the boy, and his heart, once again, twisted. He took Sebastien in his arms, as he might have done his son, if Jared had not pushed him roughly away the day his mother died. He let the boy cry. Yerin, on the other side of the room, watched but did not move. "Hush," Iddo whispered to the boy. "It will be all right."

When the boy was finished crying, Iddo turned his eyes to Yerin. "Perhaps if there were a place you could take her where she might have access to medicine," Iddo said. "Not only herbs but the kind of medicine that royal families keep in stock." He knew it was unlikely that this family could travel anywhere that medicine could be obtained, for such a thing was only possible for the wealthiest families in the kingdom of Lincastle, but he said it all the same, for hope is often an activist. He continued, to fill the empty space. "It is an aggressive lung sickness, caused by the improper circulation of the kitchen, likely, or the dirt on your floor," he said. "When the lungs breathe such things at all hours of every day, they grow sick."

Sebastien turned blazing eyes upon him and then looked away.

Oh, Sebastien looked so much like his son. It hurt terribly to look upon the boy and disappoint him so magnificently, as he clearly had. Iddo felt a pinch in his chest. He could not bear the pain, so, without another word, he left the room, left the cottage, left the small lonely yard, but something would not let him leave the path moving from the front door out of sight behind the cottage. He followed this path around to the back and saw that the bedroom where Gladys lay had one window, and it was open. He stood beside it, listening.

"We should move somewhere else," the boy was

saying. "We could go to Fairendale, somewhere her lungs could heal."

"A tropical climate is as good as any for the lungs," Yerin said.

"You do not want to go," Sebastien said. His voice turned hard. Iddo peered through the window, hoping the shadows outside hid him efficiently enough not to be discovered.

"I do not want to move your mother," Yerin said. "I fear she might die if we do." His voice broke. Yerin's eyes turned to the figure lying on the bed, sleeping.

The boy furrowed his eyebrows. "If you do not want to save my mother, then I will," he said. His hands formed into fists at his side. "It is because of you that we are here." His voice was low and tight, full of something Iddo had heard from his own son once. In the fading light, the boy's dark eyes appeared dangerously hateful. Iddo studied Sebastien's face. This boy had strong magic. He had sensed it, even noticed it before in his lessons with the boy, but never had it shown itself as clearly as this moment. Perhaps Iddo could shift their studies; he could teach the boy to use every aspect of his magic, both light and dark. It was a risky thing in the hands of the wrong pupil (and there had been a wrong pupil—a terribly wrong pupil), but perhaps the boy could handle it.

Iddo drew a bit closer to the window.

"I do not know what else to do," Yerin said. His voice shattered around the words, but his son's face did not soften even a little.

"We could steal a throne," Sebastien said. The words hung in the air between father and son. Iddo leaned closer. "You could have done that before I was born." Sebastien's eyes turned accusatory. Yerin's back slumped.

"That was never in the plans for your mother and me," Yerin said.

"It should have been," Sebastien said. "Then we would not be here." His hand gestured around the room, and his mouth twisted. "She would not be dying if you had." They were barbs to both Yerin and Iddo, but they did more than wound Iddo. They trailed a shiver down his back. In this moment, the boy was not the same boy he had known.

Iddo straightened. He would wait on the dark magic lessons. First, he would appeal to Sebastien's reason. He would bring him back to the light.

In the days after, Iddo tried to approach the boy, tried to summon him back into a seat at his teaching table, but Sebastien pulled farther away from him. He only wanted to be with his mother, and his mother was dying. Iddo could do nothing, could say nothing. He came to the cottage only for show, only for pretend. And one day, he grew weary of pretending.

"There is nothing I can do for her," he said. "There is stronger magic needed, magic I do not possess."

"Then teach me," Sebastien pleaded.

Iddo looked at the boy, whose eyes shone with desperation. "I cannot," he said. "It needs stronger magic than even you posses. Sorcerers like you and me are not permitted to keep death at bay." He cleared his throat. "But there is another. It would mean a trip."

Gladys shifted on the bed. Her eyes fluttered open. "A trip?" Her voice scratched into the walls of the room.

Sebastien leaned over his mother. "Yes, Mother," he said. "We will save your life."

"You might not survive the trip," Iddo said.

Gladys sighed. She looked at Yerin, who was standing in a corner, and Sebastien, who knelt at her side. She looked at Iddo. "I would rather die in my bed, with my family gathered around me," she said. "Thank you, Iddo, for all you have done."

Sebastien slipped from the room and slammed the front door so hard that the walls of the cottage shook.

"He will mend in time," Iddo said.

Gladys nodded, her eyes turning glassy. "Look after

him, will you?" she said. "Please? Perhaps teach him to use his magic well, as you have been doing."

"Yes," Iddo said. "I will."

Yes. He would.

Iddo moved from the house and out into the daylight that was much too bright for such a dim and gloomy conclusion. When he had almost crossed into the woods, a hand stopped him. It was Sebastien's.

"You must do something," the boy said, his voice gruff and low. "You must tell me where to go, tell me what I must do. I cannot let her die."

Iddo could see that Sebastien cared very much about his mother, but that did not change his capabilities. "There is nothing more I can do," he said. "It is beyond my abilities."

"Then you are worthless!" Sebastien said, and though Iddo knew it was only grief reaching from the boy's insides and tearing out his mouth, the words had a tangible, violent effect on his heart. It squeezed around it and would not let it go. He pressed his hand against his chest and hurried away.

Perhaps there was something he could do, if he could get the machine working. He ducked into his underground shop, careful to make sure no eyes were watching, and he lit the torch and looked at the table and tried, once more, to summon life. The magic was nowhere within him, but science did not need magic. He had built this machine, he had laid his wife upon it, and now he pulled the crank. His efforts did nothing.

He pulled the crank again and again and again, and every time it did nothing. The woman on the table did not stand up and speak.

Iddo threw his staff against the wall and watched a piece of it splinter off into the darkness.

Doors

Queen Clarion slips into the throne room. She was disturbed to see that her husband had returned to this room, that he sat on the throne and stood before a mirror, even after all she had told him and all he had decided to do. She was quite heartbroken for a moment, but a woman of action cannot remain heartbroken for long, and she soon swallowed her tears and resumed her search for information about the curse wrapped around the throne.

And she has found it, at last. That is why she is here today. She has brought the Old Man's Great Book with her, and she thrusts it in front of her, into the face of King Willis. She says the words. She lifts her staff. She waits.

And there is nothing.

No. It should have worked. It must work. What other hope is there?

She looks back at the words she said over and over and over in her mind as she walked the silent halls here. Has she said them wrong? She reads them again and holds up her staff and waits.

Nothing.

King Willis, by this time, has stood. He knocks the book from her hands. "You think you can save me with some silly book?" he says.

She backs away.

"What do you mean by coming here?" he says. "I have given orders not to allow you in this room. Page!" This King Willis has forgotten the name of his page, but still Garth comes running. "Seize her." Garth looks from the king to the queen, but before he can move, the queen shakes her head.

"I have come to break the curse," she says, loudly enough for Garth to hear it. She glances at Garth and back at the king.

"You lie," King Willis thunders, his black eyes flashing with jagged forks of lightning. "There is no curse." He reaches for her arm, but she is too quick for him. He stumbles a bit. He turns around to face her once more, his cheeks red and his eyes, if possible, darker. "Get out of my throne room."

"No," she says. "I will not leave you. You will chase me all around this throne room, and yet I will remain. I love you, Willis. And love is strong enough. It has always been strong enough."

A small crack appears in the ice locked around the king's heart—a crack that cannot be seen, only felt. But, alas, the dark magic covering both the throne and the mirror are too strong for the declarations and supplications of Queen Clarion now. It is too late. The two cursed objects have joined together, forming a cold ice so ferocious that there is no warmth that will thaw the king's heart completely or obliterate the frozen walls that confine the true king and his true memories inside a corner of his mind.

Still the queen attempts. "Remember, dear Willis. Remember who you are. Remember the children. Remember the prince."

Those memories are locked up in a prison that cannot be seen—the most dangerous kind.

The king shakes his head and thrusts out his hand, missing her once again.

"Everything you have ever said was a lie!" the king roars.

Queen Clarion dances to another corner of the

room. The king lumbers toward her. "Remember your brother, Willis. Remember Wendell. Remember the love you two shared."

Her heart pounds. *You must. You must. You must*, it says.

They continue their complicated choreography for some time, the king lunging, the queen flitting away on light feet, Garth moving forward and then retreating, as though unsure what he is expected to do. Queen Clarion does not notice the tendrils of blue mist snaking along her feet, crawling up her legs, wrapping around her. But, thankfully, Garth does. "Queen Clarion!" he shouts. "At your feet!"

She sees it then, winding its way to her chest. "No," she commands, and the moment pauses, elongates, shakes, the throne room with it. Somewhere, a clock ticks. The mist halts. Everything stills. Queen Clarion tilts her head. The king, who seems to be locked in place now, does not even blink. Queen Clarion moves toward him. She touches his arm. He still does not blink. She marvels. What is it she has done?

The mist remains outstretched, as though trapped in hasty retreat. She touches one of its cold tendrils. She lifts her staff above her head and brings it swinging down, but the mist, seemingly alive again, darts away. Her staff misses, but the mist does not reach for her again. It retracts into the mirror. Queen Clarion slams her staff against the mirror, but it does not break. She shrieks, a sound that curls the toes of Calvin in the kitchen and Garth in the room. They, too, are momentarily indisposed, but for their curling toes. It is as though time has stopped completely.

Queen Clarion rests her head against her hands, which hold her staff. She must find something that can fix what is turned in all the wrong directions. Even the sun was confused this morning, she noticed (she did not notice it the past two mornings). There must be something she can do.

She will have to leave King Willis to his throne room. She must turn her attention elsewhere for now.

But before she does…

She presses her staff against the back of her husband. He does not move. She stands as tall as she can, with a bit of help from the staff, and whispers in his ear. "Tell me where you have hidden the key to the dungeons beneath the dungeons," she says.

The answering voice does not come from the mouth of the king. It presses into her mind. It shoves down into her heart. It is the voice of her husband, the real one. Though she is surprised, she does not lift her staff from his back. "I do not know," he says. He is crying. "I do not know, Clarion. Sir Greyson took them to the dungeons." The voice falters, and then it picks up a handful of its crumbling pieces and finishes. "Please help me."

She rips the staff from him and backs away. The hulking mass of King Willis turns with daggers in his eyes. But she is out the back entrance and down the hall before he can reach out and stop her.

The book is tucked under her arm.

Her dress whispers in time with her feet as she flies down the hall, into the castle library. She locks fast the door and presses her back against it, her hands stretched out as though to keep everything outside the door out. Shaky breaths shift in and out of her chest. Sir Greyson. She must find Sir Greyson. She must ask him for help. But first, she must reconcile what she has seen with what she has heard, and this is not so very easy to do.

Sir Greyson sits at the side of his mother, brooding. She is sleeping, as she does most often now. He is sure that her time grows near. She will not be with him for much longer, so he remains by her side as often as he can, which is practically night and day, since Cora does not search for him and neither do the village people, who mostly roam about the streets with lost looks on their faces.

At least they have not retreated to their homes and the beds within them.

His mother murmurs in her sleep every now and again, and at times it is quite confounding the things she says. The day before last, she called out for his father, and when he woke her so that he might comfort her, she confessed to him that she has never believed, in all these years, that his father is dead. This startled him, for he has never considered the possibility that his father might live. His father died in Ashvale, when a Fire Mountain flung liquid flames into the sky and all over what people remained in the land, including his father. Why had she never told him that she believed his father was alive? She had not wanted to give him false hope, she had said. But a wife knows.

Sir Greyson turns these words over and over in his mind. What if his father lives? What if there is some place where he has been trapped, all these years, searching for a way out? What if the people of Ashvale did not die in a Fire Mountain but simply vanished for a time? What if Sir Greyson could find him, could find them?

How many years has it been? More than twenty since

the first Fire Mountain took his father. Almost ten since the second Fire Mountain took the brave souls who resettled Ashvale after the first. It is long enough for his father to find a way out, if he were trapped, and back to Fairendale, if he were alive. Sir Greyson tells himself that his mother's mind is not what it used to be. And this is where he ends his musings, for a knock sounds on the door and draws him from the chair in which he sits, elbows resting against his knees.

His heart flutters momentarily before his logical mind intervenes. It is not the knock of Cora. This one is too gentle. It asks a question; it does not demand. Sir Greyson moves quickly to the door and throws it open. The queen stands before him. His heart moves to his throat.

"I am sorry to disturb you, Sir Greyson," Queen Clarion says. Her blue eyes glitter. "But might you have a moment?" She glances past him, into the house, where he knows she sees his mother, for she says, "Oh." She turns her eyes back upon him.

Sir Greyson bows slightly. "Your Majesty," he says. He hesitates. He does not fancy bringing the queen into a sick house, and, besides, he has not had a chance to clean up in a few days, so he shuts the door behind him and looks up at the low gray clouds curtaining the sky.

"Perhaps a walk?" he says. He offers his arm. Queen Clarion nods and slips her own through his.

They do not speak for some minutes until Sir Greyson says, "What has brought you to our village, Your Majesty?" It feels good to say "our" village. It has been so long since this was his village.

The queen dips her head. She takes a deep breath and stops walking. She turns to Sir Greyson. "My son is safe?" Her voice is soft, but there is pain in it.

Sir Greyson swallows hard. He thinks about Cora and the blackbird she says is the prince. He nods, unable to speak.

Queen Clarion nods once.

Sir Greyson clears his throat. "If you have come for him—"

"No," Queen Clarion says. "I only want him safe, and if you can assure me that..." She fixes her eyes on Sir Greyson again. He nods again. "Then that will have to do for now." She begins to walk again, and Sir Greyson with her. "The castle is more dangerous than this village, I fear."

"Has something happened?" Sir Greyson says. His heart pounds.

Queen Clarion does not answer directly. "I am seeking a key to the dungeons beneath the dungeons," she says. Her hand presses his arm. It is as if she is consoling him when she says, "I know you are the one who delivered the children to the dungeons."

Sir Greyson looks around to see if any of the village people are out this morning. He does not want them to hear her words or his next ones. "I delivered them to the door," Sir Greyson says. "Though I did not see it."

The queen looks around as well, but perhaps for a different purpose. She leans closer to Sir Greyson and lowers her voice. "I would like to release them," she says. "I would like to find the key so that I can set them free and allow them to return to their parents." She lifts her head. Her eyes are glassy. "So that my son may be returned to me when the time is right."

Sir Greyson's gut clenches.

Something else chews along the edges of Sir Greyson's mind. "And the king would like the same?" he says. And his heart beats, *Yes, please. Yes, please. Yes, please.*

Queen Clarion straightens her back. Her eyes shift away from Sir Greyson's. "The king is not himself," she says. "He is under the influence of some…" She searches for a word. "Power." Her eyes slide back to Sir Greyson's. "It is not him who makes the decisions, you see."

"Influence," Sir Greyson says, reveling in the word, for it means he was correct all along. He has always known there was some goodness in King Willis. It is what he has tried to tell Cora.

Queen Clarion clears her throat. "It is too much to consider for now," she says. "I am only concerned, at the moment, with freeing the children. And I need your help."

"But without the king's consent," Sir Greyson says.

Queen Clarion draws herself up to her full height, which is nearly even with Sir Greyson's chin. She is about the same size as Cora. "I am a queen," she says. "I can make my own decisions."

It is not how things are done in the kingdom of Fairendale, but Sir Greyson does not point this out. In the last days and weeks, he has been in the near-constant presence of another strong woman. And he sees the same spark in Queen Clarion's eyes that flashes in Cora's. She will persist. This he knows.

But he will have to disappoint her first. "I do not know where the key is," he says. "I walked the children to the door, and Cook's assistant, Calvin, took them below. I did not even see the door." He searches the recesses of his mind for a moment. "I do not believe the boy had a key either."

Queen Clarion lets out a breath. Her height diminishes slightly, as though she is deflating right before his eyes. "Well," she says. "It is as I feared." She arches one perfect eyebrow at him. "And you would tell me if you knew?" she says.

She does not quite trust him, and he cannot blame her. But still, it is a barb in his chest.

"I would," he says, and his voice wobbles. He feels that perhaps he should say more, so he does. "I would do anything to free the children. Anything. A dungeon is no place for children."

Queen Clarion stares at him for a moment. Her eyes darken and then grow glassy. She dips her head again, never taking her eyes from his. "Thank you for your service, Sir Greyson," she says. "It is most appreciated. No captain should ever have to endure what you have endured, and you have done it with the utmost honor and integrity." She takes a step closer to him and places her other hand, the one that does not clutch his arm, on his fist, which is clenched in an effort to keep at bay the emotions that her unexpected words have drawn forth from his depths. "I know your kind. I know that you will save Fairendale, in your own way." Warmth blooms in his chest and rises up to his face and his eyes. He wipes his cheeks.

"I am sorry I could not help you more," he says, and he truly is.

Queen Clarion smiles then, a beautiful, shining light of a smile. "I know you are," she says. "But there is a boy."

"Yes," he says. "A boy."

"A boy," she says. "A boy who feeds the children, even now. He has been through the door."

"Calvin," Sir Greyson says.

"Yes. Calvin." The queen pats his hand once more and then backs away from him. "I must return to the castle now. I must see about finding that door." And then she turns and runs away so quickly that Sir Greyson cannot tell her of the legends that surround the dungeons beneath the dungeons, the ones that say only one person is permitted through the door. He watches her grow smaller in the distance, her golden hair flying behind her in her haste.

And when he returns to the cottage where his mother sleeps, it is a different sort of brooding that he does. It is a brooding that considers, from every angle, how the kingdom of Fairendale might be saved from its graying death. He becomes, in his brooding, a Captain of the Queen's Guard.

It did not take Cook long to get the castle kitchen back on track. In fact, it has only required a day's work. So far, Cook has prepared every meal, filled the root cellar, revitalized the gardens, cleaned the grime from walls and surfaces and floors, and, perhaps most importantly, reinstated her spell of protection. Calvin observes everything Cook does, though some of it is mysterious. He does not know why, for example, when he watched her last eve, she stood at the front doors of the castle, touching the brass bear knocker with her right hand. He saw the brass knocker glow. He saw it speak. He did not hear what it said, for he was too far away, and there were too many night sounds—hoots and shrieks and rumbles. He could feel the eyes of a hundred creatures, watching him. He only stayed for a few moments, and then he raced back into the cover of his room, behind the safe, stone walls of the castle.

Cook, strangely, has taken to announcing a meal before Garth serves it, as though the king is one of many seated at the long wooden dining table. The king seems amused by this, and Calvin wonders why Cook feels the need to do it, though he must admit that it puts him into a mind of greater days. He was not at the castle during the merry days of the Good King Brendon, nor was Cook, but he suspects she does what she does to honor those days. They were lighter, more extravagant, full of hope. At least that is what the stories say. He wonders if the castle will ever again see a dining table filled with people, rather than just a king.

The queen takes most of her meals in the castle library now. They hardly see her.

Today, Calvin has filled another large basket with vegetables and stolen candles. He arranges it around a wide black pot that holds last night's thick and hearty soup. He hopes that it will nourish the children in a way his meals never did.

He packs it all right in front of Cook. He is, in truth, still rather angry with her, and he dares her, as only a boy can do, to say something. She does not, however. She eyes him a couple of times and even once kneels at his side to secure the pot with a few more towels and then turns her back.

Calvin, not for the first time, marvels. Had he known so little about Cook while she was here? Or had he simply not noticed? He shakes his head and picks up the basket.

He does not, alas, remember that he promised Garth a trip into the dungeons beneath the dungeons until he is just past the secret door. His arms already ache, and he does not want to turn around. He will make his apologies and bring Garth next time. It is unfortunate that he forgot, for he could have used the help delivering the supplies. The candle grinds between his teeth. He shakes his head, and the flame flickers and nearly goes out. He breathes a sigh of relief when it does not, and it dances wildly again in the wake of his expelled air.

He lets out a growl and moves on his way before he loses the light by his own silly errors.

"You come again," Yerin says when Calvin rounds the corner. The prophet's wrinkles fold into a smile.

"I have brought much for you today," Calvin says. "Some news as well."

He slides the bowls through the iron bars while Yerin returns those he left on his last visit. He hands out the vegetables and the bread and then ladles out the soup into six bowls. He waits until some children have eaten and fills the bowls again. And again. And again.

It is the first time the children have had full bellies, and Calvin feels the warmth of satisfaction expand in his own belly, as if he, too, has eaten his fill.

"And you," Calvin says, filling a bowl once more and pushing it toward Yerin.

"They need it more than I do," Yerin says, and he begins to hand the bowl to Agnes.

"I can eat no more," she says, her voice skipping like

music notes on the air.

The children around her agree.

"You must eat," Calvin says, and the children agree again.

So Yerin does. He closes his eyes after the first bite. His eyes remain closed while he chews. "You have done well," he says when he has finished.

"I did not cook it," Calvin says. "Cook has returned."

Yerin sets down the bowl. "She has returned?" he says.

"She walked out of the woods two days ago," Calvin says. "I do not know where she went, but she is back." Even now, as he says these words for perhaps the hundredth time—for he had to repeat them to himself on the first evening so he would believe them—he feels a burst of hope. Agnes beams at him, and, for the first time, he beams right back, though she cannot see it.

A scuttling in the corner turns him toward shadows. As always, it is the shadows of the three mice that emerge first, long and monstrous along the back wall.

"We have found nothing," the first mouse says. Calvin still cannot tell them apart.

"Nothing," the second mouse says.

The third mouse grunts.

"What are you trying to find?" Calvin says.

"We have been searching the castle library," the first mouse says.

"For some parchment," the second mouse says. "And a book."

The third mouse points at Yerin.

"We found nothing," the first mouse says.

"Not the parchment, and not the book," says the second mouse.

"Nothing, Timmy," says the first. Gus. There are only two mice who talk: Gus and Timmy. Florence is the one who says nothing at all.

Calvin is quite proud of his powers of deduction.

"What book are you trying to find?" Calvin says. He turns toward the prophet.

"The Old Man's Great Book," Yerin says. "I thought that it would, perhaps, have information about a key. But we are unable to find the book."

"Perhaps I can look for it," Calvin says, and then another thought enters his mind. "Perhaps Cook will know where it is."

"It would be a great help to the cause, dear boy," Yerin says.

Calvin nods. He can do this thing, now that Cook had returned.

"It is a magical book," Yerin says. "It talks when

coaxed. It will magically open to the page for which you are looking. It restores gifts of magic." Yerin draws closer to the iron bars, his eyes piercing Calvin's. "It is a valuable book."

The words seem to be a warning of some sort. Calvin nods. "I will handle it with care," he says. "If I find it."

"It is all you can do," Yerin says.

Calvin says his goodbyes and turns to go, bounding up the stairs in utter darkness and bursting through the secret door in a rush of relief. He collides with Queen Clarion and would perhaps have fallen back down the steep stairs, if not for the secret door that became, instead, a sealed up wall. He falls against it with such force that it steals his breath for some moments.

The queen rushes toward him. "Forgive me," the queen says.

Of course he does.

"You know where the entrance is," she says. She slides her hands along the wall behind him, searching.

Calvin's throat is too clogged up to speak. He has been found out. He does not know much about this queen, but he fears that she will tell the king, and then it will all be over. He will not be able to help the children.

"Tell me," she says, the pitch of her voice rising in desperation. "Please." The word breaks in two, and the queen turns her glassy eyes to him.

"Yes, I know where it is," Calvin says, for he has seen something in her eyes, and it is not malice.

"Show me," she says. Calvin stands and turns. He reaches for the latch, but it is not there. He moves slightly to the right and reaches again. It is not there. He moves to the left and repeats his actions. "It is no longer here," he says, turning to face the queen again. His mind is muddled with confusion. Why would the door disappear?

Queen Clarion's shoulders sag, along with her beautiful head. Calvin stares at the gleaming crown. The jewels wink at him. She lifts her head again. "It is an enchanted door?" she says.

"I do not know," Calvin says.

"An invisible one," Queen Clarion says.

"It has never been invisible to me," Calvin says.

Queen Clarion tilts her head slightly. Her eyes reach through and beyond him. She is thinking. She murmurs to herself. He cannot hear it. Then her eyes focus back on his face. "There is a spell," she says. "It allows a door to show itself only to one person." She lets the words dangle between them. Calvin does not know what to say. "Do you know what that means, Calvin?"

He shakes his head. "No," he says.

The queen smiles momentarily, but it slips quickly

from her lips, lost on a tide of worries that darken her eyes. "It means that the door chose you, Calvin. It chose you to care for the children. You are the only one who can."

This knowledge feels heavy on his shoulders and yet large inside his chest. It is both a terrifying thing and a wonderful thing to be chosen.

"I do not understand," Calvin says, for he still does not understand completely.

Queen Clarion bends so that she is eye level with him. Calvin pushes away the urge to look at the ground, as he so often does when eyes are turned his way. "It means that you are the only one who can save them," she says.

"I cannot save them without a key," Calvin says. "And I do not know where that key is."

The queen's eyes hold his for a moment, and then they blink rapidly as she looks back toward the place where the door had been. She straightens. "Nor do I," she says. "But when we find it, you will be the one to set them free." He feels her eyes on him again. "You are needed for this."

It is difficult to explain what the words of the queen have done to a serving boy. There is the fact that the queen used "we" when referring to who would find the key. Calvin knows, now, that he is not alone in his search. And there is the important phrase, "You are needed." Calvin has not been needed for very much in his short life. Of course he was needed to hold down the castle in Cook's absence, but she has returned, and he is no longer needed in such a dire way.

But he is needed for this, and this he shall do.

"I do not know where to begin looking for a key," Calvin says. "Do you?"

The queen stares at the wall that is supposed to hold a secret door. She shakes her head. "But there are books," she says. "I will read them all if I must." She does not look at Calvin, but she reaches for his hand, and he willingly gives it to his queen. "I will help you, Calvin. We will free the children."

The queen squeezes his hand between her fingers, and then she turns and walks away with hardly a sound, only the whisper of her skirts.

As soon as she is gone, the secret door reappears. Calvin tilts his head, touches it, and opens it, just to be sure. He shakes his head.

Sometimes magic is quite confounding.

It is unfortunate, dear reader, that Calvin forgets all about the Old Man's Great Book as he moves down and through the castle halls, back on his way to the castle kitchen, where Cook awaits him.

In the morning, Oscar enters the inn's dining hall, fully expecting that he will not be given leave to dine. But the innkeeper serves him and says that his stay has been fully paid for. He is entitled to three warm meals a day, and he is free to remain as long as he needs. Oscar is in quite a good mood as he ambles through the village streets and out toward the shore, where he has agreed to meet Princess Freya, although neither of them set a time. He has brought his book, however, and he settles himself beneath a tree and begins to read.

After a time, he sits looking at the water. It is a glistening sight. He supposes this is the lure of the land of Lincastle, the violet waters awaiting swimmers, the golden sand shimmering in the sun, the sound of birds luring those who listen into a trance of peace. He could tell his mother about this part of Lincastle. It is the lovely part.

"It is not often I see people sitting along the beach, in complete silence," a voice says. Oscar knows without turning to look that it is Princess Freya.

"I like the calm voice of the sea," Oscar says. "The

way it whispers secrets and then pulls away."

"That is a lovely image," Princess Freya says. She drops down next to him. She smells of honey and rose. She is wearing a high-collared dress in pink silk today. The dress will be dirty when she rises from the sand, and he worries about this for a small amount of time before the worrying turns, as all his thoughts inevitably turn, to his mother. When he was a small boy, Oscar used to thrust his hands in the dark brown earth of Fairendale and let it cover every inch of him. His mother used to make him wash in the cove when he did it. He always loved the part where he got dirty, but he hated the part where he must wash in the cove, for the mermaids were always waiting. He had read far too many stories about mermaids to feel even remotely comfortable in their presence. Even now, thinking of mermaids, he shivers.

"Cold?" says Princess Freya. Her voice holds concern and a slight tinge of confusion. It is warm and wet in the land of Lincastle. "We could move out into the sunlight."

"No," he says. "I was thinking of mermaids."

"Mermaids," Princess Freya says. "I have read of mermaids, but I have never seen one."

"You would not want to see one," Oscar says. "They are very like the stories written about them."

"Pointy teeth?" Princess Freya says.

"So many of them," Oscar says.

"But beautiful faces?" Princess Freya says.

"Until they open their mouths," Oscar says. He shivers again.

"Your land must have had many mermaids for you to have seen them," Princess Freya says. "I live near the sea, and I have not seen one."

Oscar's heart pounds. Does she know something of Fairendale that he does not know? Fairendale is—was, perhaps—the most beautiful of all the lands, but does that mean it had more mermaids than most? He swallows hard and says what he hopes is true: "No more than most."

Princess Freya does not answer. They sit in silence for a time, until the princess looks at him out of the corner of her eye.

"You remind me of my father," she says. "He has a serious disposition and loves books."

Oscar is suddenly, unexplainably, angry about her inference—that he could be anything like a royal person, like a king. He looks at the sand and lets a handful slip through his fingers. "You know nothing about my sort of life," he says, the words harsher than he intends. But his thoughts whirl and spin and then settle on his mother, who worked hard to procure every book she brought to her shop, and his friends, who swept the village streets and washed the shop windows and wore boots with holes in them. He stares sullenly at his brand new boots that practically glow, even when in the shade.

"I did not mean to anger you," Princess Freya says. Her hand on his arm is warm and soft.

Oscar shakes his head, ashamed at his outburst. "I am sorry," he says.

"No," Princess Freya says. "You have no reason to apologize. I know you are here alone." Oscar's eyes move to hers. "Where is your family?" she says. "Where are the people who love you?" She turns toward him and takes both of his hands in hers. "What is your land? It is not this one, that much is plain to me."

Oscar withdraws his hands from hers. "Thank you for the boots," he says. He stands.

"Please do not go," Princess Freya says. She stands as well. "I will not ask you any more questions. Only stay."

Oscar looks at her for a very long time. He looks into those eyes, such a beautiful shade of blue, and after a moment, he sees her. He sees her loneliness, her longing, her hope. He sees that she needs him as much as he needs her.

He nods once and sits again.

Princess Freya turns to a small diamond-studded bag

that sits beside her. "I brought you another book," she says. "I thought you might read the other quickly and need something else to occupy your mind." She pulls out a very thick red leather book. "Have you read this one?"

Oscar takes the book from her and runs his hand along the title. *The Enchanting Stories of Lincastle*, scrawled in golden script. He has never even seen this book. He smiles. "No," he says.

"It is read to every child in Lincastle before their tenth birthday," Princess Freya says. "There are some frightening tales in it, intended to keep us away from the Violet Sea."

"I shall read it with great interest," Oscar says.

"I am sure you shall," Princess Freya says, and her smile is nearly as bright as the sun. "I should like to know what you think of it. My great-grandmother wrote it."

"She was a scribe?" Oscar says. "A royal scribe?"

"My family has some interesting people in it," Princess Freya says. "Long ago, one of my great-grandfathers discovered this land."

Oscar turns toward her now, unable to hide his interest. "You are a granddaughter of Dale Enderling, the founder of Fairendale?"

Princess Freya nods. "Somewhere along the line," she says. "He was the first king of Lincastle. The castle has been in my family for many, many years."

Oscar looks back at the book in his hands. His heart pounds. He wants to open it now and read it, and, as though she senses his irrepressible desire, Princess Freya says, "Will you read one of them to me?" And Oscar cracks open the book, which smells of age and wonder, and begins to read.

He reads three stories instead of one, and then Princess Freya lays her hand on his arm and he looks up. The day has grown late, and Oscar's belly feels hollow. "I must go," Princess Freya says. "But we will meet tomorrow? Here?"

"Yes," Oscar says. He will look forward to it.

He watches her until she is swallowed by the extravagant houses of an extravagant people, and then he turns his attention back to the storybook in his hands, his hollow belly forgotten in the spell of a story.

Work

Iddo was there when Gladys took her last breath.

There is a strangeness to someone dying. It does not happen in an instant, as you might suppose. It happens gradually, in a breath and then another and still another. The sound becomes raspy, splintered. Gladys coughed, opened her eyes, and looked at her son with a gaze so steady and alive one might have thought the sickness had resolved itself completely. "You will be all right, my love," she said, and then there was nothing. The air that had moved in and out of her chest simply vanished. The strength that had momentarily lifted her head let it fall with a gentle whisper. There was no other sound but Sebastien's wounded howl, which grew louder and louder in the small room. Yerin took his son in his arms, but Sebastien ripped away from him and fell desperately on top of his mother's body. He shook her, begged her to wake. Iddo put a hand on the boy's shoulder, but Sebastien twisted away and stood to his feet. For a moment, he looked at the two men with such hatred that Iddo shuddered. And then he ran from the room. Iddo heard him stumble a time or two, but he made it out the door, and the house grew silent once again.

Iddo remained as he was for quite some time. Yerin did not go after his son, and Iddo did not feel it was his place to do so. He had lost many important people in his life, and perhaps he could have shared this with the boy, but new grief, he knew, was in no position to listen yet. He wished he could erase the boy's pain. He wished the machine would work. Sorrow stung the back of his nose.

"I am sorry for your loss," Iddo said to Yerin, and he truly meant it.

Yerin looked up at him. His eyes were rimmed in red but the deepest blue Iddo had ever seen. They were like the night sky, just before the moon begins to glow in earnest. Had he ever seen eyes as sad as Yerin's were in that moment? Perhaps if he had looked into a mirror, yes, he would have.

"I will take the body and prepare it for burial, if you wish," Iddo said. While it was the responsibility of a Healer to prepare bodies for burial, this one was different. It called to him. It said, *Try again.* And he could do nothing but listen. He would try again to raise life from the dead—for Yerin, for the boy, for himself.

"Perhaps you might come back later," Yerin said. His voice was soft, almost a whisper. "I would like some time with her."

"Yes," Iddo said. "I understand." He put a hand on Yerin's shoulder and squeezed it. He departed the room silently.

The boy was standing in the doorway of the cottage. He would not let Iddo pass. His face twisted up in sorrow and disappointment and something else that Iddo could not read, not entirely. "I cannot believe you both did nothing for my mother," Sebastien said, his words piercing Iddo like daggers, all along the front of his chest. Iddo lifted his arms, as though to protect himself. The boy appeared dangerous, and he had the gift of magic. It was right for Iddo to be afraid.

"There was nothing to be done, my dear child," Iddo said. "I do not posses the kind of magic that can keep away death."

Sebastien looked at him and lifted his chin. His stature was befitting a prince. "You could have helped me," he said, and Iddo felt the change. There was a dark sadness, yes, but there was also a burning rage that snaked toward Iddo. "You could have convinced my father to do something. You could have taught me healing magic. You could have introduced me to the dark."

Iddo shook his head. "No," he said, and the breath he released was long and weary. "I am afraid I do not heal with magic anymore." He had never told anyone this. He wondered if it was the right time to tell anyone now. He lowered his voice, in case Yerin was listening. "I heal only with science."

The boy stared at him, his mouth pulling open. "Science?" he said. "What is science to magic?"

"It is everything," Iddo said, "when it is all you have left."

Sebastien glared at him, his eyes smoldering. But when he spoke, his voice was weak, a child's. "Your science could not save my mother," he said. His shoulders slumped a bit.

"I can see you loved her very much," Iddo said.

"What do you know of love?" Sebastien's words scraped Iddo's face. "What do you know of loss?" They clawed and bruised.

Iddo closed his eyes for a moment, but he did not tell the boy what he knew of love, of loss. He only said, "I am sorry," and attempted to slide past the boy.

But Sebastien rushed at him, meeting Iddo's chest with his clenched fists, pounding, beating, damaging. And though the prophet was old, he was not weak. He took the boy's hands in his own and said, against his own good judgment, "Perhaps there is something we might do." This stilled the boy's hands, and Iddo glanced furtively behind him, to ensure that Yerin was not standing in the doorway, listening. Yerin did not emerge from the room where his wife's body lay.

"Tell me," Sebastien said. The tears rolled down his face and pooled on the neck of his tunic. "Tell me what I can do. Tell me it is not too late."

"It must be our secret," Iddo said, drawing the boy outside the cottage.

The boy looked at him, and all the fight had gone out of him.

"Here is what I shall do." Iddo leaned close to Sebastien and lowered his voice to a whisper. "I shall come for your mother's body. I have been working on a machine that will bring the dead back to life. I need a bit of time, but I believe…" He did not finish. It was enough to say that he believed. He believed he could do it. He believed it would work. He believed.

He cleared his throat. "You must let me take her body. And when it is time for the burial, if I have not yet succeeded, you must pretend the body that is lowered into the ground is hers."

Sebastien lifted his eyes to Iddo. The two stared at one another for some minutes. At last Sebastien nodded his head. "Very well," he said. And then again. "Very well."

"I shall return later," Iddo said. "When the time for grieving is done."

And he did. Later that evening, Iddo brought a horse and a cart and a dozen or so blankets so that he could cover the body he would carry to his own cottage. It was considered ill fortune for others to look upon a dead body that was not one of their own. No one in Lincastle liked to even admit that death was a real possibility, though it came for everyone.

When Iddo had placed the body, already wrapped in blankets, on the cart and spread the remainder of the blankets over it, he turned to Yerin and Sebastien. The boy's lips trembled, and, in a sudden rush of anguish, Sebastien ran, vanishing inside the cover of the trees. Iddo watched him go, as he had once watched his own son go, and turned sympathetic eyes to Yerin.

"It is the same for every boy who loses his mother," Iddo said, though he did not say how he knew it. He shook off the heavy cloak of sorrow. It did not do to dwell on sorrow, especially one so heavy.

Yerin merely nodded his head.

"It will pass in time," Iddo said, though he was unsure whether he believed his own words. Did great, gutting loss ever pass in time? Did one always walk around with a gaping, bleeding hole in one's heart? Did one limp through life ever after?

Yerin began to walk toward the woods where his son had disappeared. "Perhaps you should let the boy grieve in his own way," Iddo said. And Yerin's steps halted. He turned back toward the cottage and sighed.

"Yes," he said. "I suppose it is all that is left to do."

And because there was nothing else to say, Iddo led his horse, which pulled the cart with the body of Gladys, away toward his cottage, or, more precisely, toward the secret work space where his machine waited for another test subject.

He had two days before the burial ceremony. Surely he could succeed with two days, could he not? What would they think if instead of a body prepared for burial he presented to them a living woman?

The boy would become more than his student. He would become his son.

Iddo took out his tools and began to work.

Dangers

The next morning, before the settled-upon time Oscar and Princess Freya had agreed to meet one another at the seaside, Oscar ventures into the village again, hopeful that its people, absorbed in their own lives, will have forgotten his face. He suspects that they will not remember him at all, for this is the weakness of superficial people.

He buttons his cloak at the neck, wraps it around him so as to appear more stately, and wrinkles his nose at a hole near the left corner, as though he can make it disappear with his derision. It remains.

Oscar spies Princess Freya on the edge of the village closest to the castle. She is waving goodbye to a man who must be her father, for he wears a large golden crown on his head. Its jewels sparkle in the early morning light. He bends down and kisses her cheek before lifting himself onto the back of a gleaming white horse. She lifts her hand as he gallops away, toward the castle, but he does not look back. Princess Freya remains standing, staring. Oscar ventures closer, until he draws even with her.

They do not speak for some moments. The wind lifts her hair and tangles its dark edges. She hardly notices.

"What is it?" Oscar says at last, unable to continue standing in the tight silence that surrounds them.

"He is going to see some of the other kingdoms," Princess Freya says.

"Oh," Oscar says, and he tries to hide the alarm in his voice, but he has never been successful at hiding what he feels. Princess Freya looks at him out of the corner of her eyes.

"The relationship between the other kingdoms has become…" Princess Freya searches for a word.

"Tense?" Oscar says.

Princess Freya lets out a breath. "Yes," she says. "Tense. Perhaps a stronger word than tense."

"Why?" Oscar says.

"There is a reward out for some magical children," Princess Freya says. She does not look at him. He does not say anything, though he can feel his cheeks warming.

"You are one of the lost children of Fairendale,"

Princess Freya says, and it is not a question at all. It is a sure statement of fact. "You have come to Lincastle from the land of Fairendale." Her voice holds wonder and awe. "You escaped from the king."

Oscar glances behind him and to both sides, to ensure that no one is listening without permission. His voice is very low when he says, "Yes. I did come from the land of Fairendale."

"So you have the gift of magic," Princess Freya says, again a statement rather than a question.

"No," Oscar says. "I was not born with the gift of magic. The king does not only hunt magical children. He hunts all the children of Fairendale." And then it all comes spilling out—the injustice of the king, the imprisonment of all the children, the hopelessness of an eventual return to his home. All the pieces he has carried into the Weeping Woods, into the dragon lands of Morad and now, here, to Lincastle.

Princess Freya's eyes have widened during the tale. "How horrible," she says. "It is not what the king's letter suggested."

"There is a letter?" Oscar says.

"Yes," Princess Freya says. "It is why my father desires to visit the other kingdoms. The king of Fairendale is demanding that all children be turned over to him so that he can find the lost ones."

"He will not return the ones who do not belong to Fairendale," Oscar says. "It is not the way of our king."

"My father does not plan to obey the king's wishes," Princess Freya says. "It is why he rides to the other lands, to see who might join him in his resistance." She takes in a deep breath and lets it out again. "The king of Fairendale is demanding that all the children in every kingdom be turned over to him, particularly those between the ages of eleven and twelve." She looks at Oscar. "I am twelve. It is why my father is angry. I am a princess. I have my own kingdom already. I am not interested in that of Fairendale." She stares at her hands, the silence lifting and twirling between them like a ribbon on the wind. She nearly says something twice and then stops. Finally, she says, as though to herself, "There must be a reason for the king's demands."

"The king is mad," Oscar says, before he can stop the words.

"Perhaps we do not know the entire story," Princess Freya says. "You have read the stories of this land, have you not?"

Yes. Oscar read the entire book yesterday. He could not stop even when it grew too dark inside his room to read. He simply lit a candle and read until it burned away.

"There is dark magic in this land," Princess Freya says. "Ancient magic that has not been seen in a very long time. Magic that twists people's hearts and makes them become what they were not born to become." She pauses. "My grandmother believed in this magic. And they called her mad."

Oscar shivers. "People are who they are," he says. "And nothing more."

Princess Freya shakes her head. "It is much more complicated than that, I think."

"You are too kind," Oscar says. "You are not even real." He begins to walk away, though he cannot say exactly why. He is inexplicably angry at the hope that shines out from her eyes, angry at the words she has said —words that seem to excuse King Willis from his obsession.

Princess Freya does not allow him to leave, however. She places a hand on his arm, and his insides wrench.

"Do not go, Oscar," she says. "It is not safe."

"I will be just fine," he says.

"But you are a twelve-year-old boy," she says. "You are one of the lost children. It is only a matter of time before the people of Lincastle understand this. And then you will have nowhere to go."

"What is it you suggest, then?" he says.

"Stay at the castle," she says.

"And what would your father say to housing a lost child of Fairendale?" Oscar says.

A shadow slides into her eyes, curls up, and stares out at him. "It is not my father we must convince," she says. "It is his closest advisor. Von Albeck." She seems to consider this, thinking out loud. "It will not work yet. I need more time."

"I will return to my room," Oscar says.

"I suppose that would be best," Princess Freya says. She brightens considerably. "But you have braved the Wishing Woods."

"The Wishing Woods?" Oscar says, confused all around. First, why would she brighten at such a random observation, and, second, the Wishing Woods?

Princess Freya tilts her head. "Yes. Did you not know the name of the woods around Lincastle?"

"No," he says. "I thought they were all called the Weeping Woods."

"We all have our own names for the forest that surrounds and divides our lands," Princess Freya says. "I am surprised you did not read it in your geography books. Or absorb it from my grandmother's book. She did call the woods by their name, did she not?"

Oscar knows she is teasing him, so he smiles, though he does not much feel like smiling. He says what he is thinking. "The king of Fairendale will stop at nothing."

Princess Freya lifts her chin. "My father is brave," she says. "And he has many men who love him, not only in this land but in all the others. The king of Fairendale cannot possibly win. He will not have the children. He will not have you."

Oscar swallows his fear and nods.

"Did you know that there is a monster in the Wishing Woods?" Princess Freya says.

"It is not in the stories," Oscar says.

"The monster came to us more recently," Princess Freya says. "She has not been seen since before I was born, but my father knows her stories. She was said to look like a woman who had been raised from the dead."

Oscar shivers again.

"It is a good thing you are staying at the inn," Princess Freya says. "Though how you managed in an old storage shelter, I do not know." She smiles at him. "You must be very brave."

Oscar shakes his head. "No," he says. "I have never been brave. Only desperate."

Princess Freya does not answer. She turns toward the beach, watching the birds dip and soar. "We use our birds as messengers," she says. "My father could have done the same, but he wanted to go himself."

"You are afraid for him," Oscar says.

"As most daughters would be," Princess Freya says. "I do not like it when my father is gone from the castle. I feel…" She seems to search for a word again.

"Exposed," Oscar says.

"Yes," she says, glancing at him. "Not many like the thought of a princess inheriting the throne." She shrugs, her blue eyes soft and glassy. "But I am his only child."

Oscar says nothing.

The birds swoop and glide. "I have always wanted to fly like the birds," Princess Freya says. "Ever since I was a little girl."

And Oscar is overcome by a desire to make her wings. To give her what she most desires. But he only smiles. "Man—or woman—cannot fly," he says.

"Yes, I know," she says. "My father told me many times. Fortunately, I never tried."

They laugh, hers like a joyful bell chiming on the wind.

"Well," she says. "I must return to the castle. My mother will be waiting for me. She gets quite sad when my father is gone." She turns to Oscar. "I will not be able to meet this afternoon." And before he can respond, she leans forward and kisses his cheek.

His cheek flames, but it is nothing to the flames that torch his heart.

She is gone before he can find his words.

Arthur and Zorag have been awake for several hours. Zorag slept fitfully within the bounds of Gyria, but Arthur had the most restful sleep he has had in some time, which is why he is quite cheerful this morning.

To be honest, he is also feeling cheerful for the simple fact that no dragons have shown themselves. Arthur is beginning to think they do not exist in this land anymore. Zorag insists that he smells them, but what few stories exist of Ashvale always tell of a land that smells of armpits and flatulence. Arthur thinks that perhaps the dragon is only smelling the natural stench of the land.

"We must go deeper," Zorag says.

Arthur sighs. He had hoped that would not be the case. If they go deeper into the land, they will likely come in direct contact with a Fire Mountain, which Zorag says is really a dragon. Arthur is not, by nature, doubtful, but dragons mistaken for Fire Mountains? This is difficult to believe, even for him. He has more faith in the human race to open their eyes and see the fantastical than he does in Zorag's theory.

Because he knows the stories of Ashvale's destruction, Arthur is terribly afraid of Fire Mountains. Zorag has assured him that if a Fire Moutain erupts while they walk the land, they will lift into the sky before its red liquid can even touch the ground. This is a slight consolation to Arthur; as long as he is on the back of the dragon, he shall remain safe.

Unless, of course, those Fire Mountains can fly.

Arthur shivers again and holds tighter to Zorag's spines.

The land looks much different in the light of the morning than it did at dusk. A thick, heavy fog hides the distant Fire Mountains from view. As the dragon moves through it, the water particles, which are black with Fire Mountain dust, cling to Zorag's scales and Arthur's clothes in dirty drops. At some point the sun burns away some of the mist, and their way becomes clearer, but not completely. The haze, it seems, is an ever-present quality of this land. Arthur squints his eyes. Are the mountains different this morning? Have they changed position? He did not study them well enough last eve to truly tell.

He coughs.

"Try not to breathe the dust," Zorag says.

Arthur does not know how he can manage that. The dust is everywhere. He breathes shallowly, but his lungs grope for more air.

After an hour or so of slow travel, Zorag and Arthur pass a small tributary that cracks in half, snaking off in two directions, then three. Arthur has nearly exhausted his water supply, so he slides off the back of the dragon and approaches the stream. He bends and reaches, but Zorag's voice stops him from touching.

"Do not fill your leather here," Zorag says. "Those who are not accustomed to this kind of water can become gravely ill if they drink it. Or worse." Arthur crouches back on his heels and brushes his hands on his wet breeches. When he pulls his hands away, they are covered in black dust. The water, too, holds large particles of dust. He can see that now. It is not clear like the tributaries in Fairendale.

"I must find water soon," Arthur says. He swishes what is left in his leather container. He takes a small sip.

"We are nearly done with this land," Zorag says. His eyes flick around. "I had thought they would show themselves before now."

"Perhaps they have abandoned the land," Arthur says. "Perhaps the Fire Mountains—"

Zorag does not allow him to finish. "The Fire

Mountains *are* the dragons," he says. "They simply do not wish to engage. So we cannot remain." He gazes out on the land with his golden eyes. "It would be too dangerous."

Three Fire Mountains puff rings of smoke at once. Arthur studies them to see if there is any sort of pattern, but the smoke vanishes too quickly. The land is eerily silent, except for the occasional whoosh from a Fire Mountain and an accompanying rumble of the ground. The sulfuric smell—blended expertly with the sort of stench that might radiate from an armpit that has not been washed in a week—has grown nearly unbearable. Arthur's nose burns. He would like to leave the land of Gyria—sooner rather than later.

Zorag bends so that Arthur can climb on his back again. But before Arthur can manage, the ground gives a shake—one so violent that Arthur loses his balance and stumbles backward. He throws out a hand to catch himself. A finger touches the murky tributary, and his skin burns, stings, melts. He withdraws his hand quickly, but his finger is red and scalded. He does not cry out.

There is a good reason he does not cry out, though the pain is agonizing. A dragon stands before Zorag. It looks as though it has been carved out of bronze stone. Its eye is a green slit.

"Why are you in this land?" The dragon speaks, and the ground shifts, a crack opening in front of Arthur. He steps back. "Why have you brought a human here?" The dragon blinks, and his face comes alive with green slits glowing and blinking at Zorag and Arthur. Arthur cannot even count the number of eyes. He shrinks a bit and moves closer to Zorag, though he knows he could never hide from so many eyes.

"We have come seeking help," Zorag says. He bows his head.

The dragon pulls up to his full height, his bronze belly shimmering in the sun that has momentarily shattered the haze.

"Who dares trespass on the land that is ours?" Another dragon appears, as tall as the first, but with scales of a slightly duller tint, all copper and rust. This one has a single blue eye, but Arthur, now that he knows how to look, sees the many eyes placed at random upon the dragon's fearsome head. This dragon wears a thick layer of dust on his back. Arthur glances at the horizon. It has changed. He is sure of it. The Fire Mountains have moved. The dragons are gathering.

The first dragon with the green eyes extends his wings to their full capacity. He is about four times as large as Zorag—four hundred feet wide or more. Arthur's jaw drops. The dragon's bronze wings look rusted, green growing along the edges. His claws, attached to the ends of the wings, snap. Arthur places a hand on Zorag, as though to remind the dragon that he is still on the ground should Zorag be considering a quick escape into the sky. But Zorag does not even flinch.

Arthur gazes at Zorag and then back at the two dragons. The larger one, the one with the glowing green eye, has two bronze horns growing out the top of his head, positioned perfectly above his two predominant eyes. What appears to be a bronze beard extends from his chin. He stares at Zorag with one eye and Arthur with all the others.

"Those who trespass," the dragon says, "should prepare to die."

Arthur, for the second time in too few weeks, feels a deep and dark terror flare across his body.

The Enchantress has taken to carrying the extra staffs she has collected from the two formerly lost and now recovered magical girls of Fairendale, because she does not trust staffs laid in carts, jostled by travel. She assumes that she might be able to place some sort of enchantment on the staffs, to bind their magic into their wood, but she does not know how one would disassemble that spell, and she does not want to risk stealing magic from two magical girls, if it is possible not to. So, for now, she carries them.

It is slow going, however, with two staffs that she cannot compress into smaller items. They do not belong to her, so she cannot make them do anything magical. They are so cumbersome that for the last several minutes she has been considering attempting to turn the two blackbirds who represent the magical girls—she is not even sure which blackbird is which child anymore—back into their human form, but she does not want to risk trying and failing in front of the Huntsman. Though they have captured five of the lost children of Fairendale and she has transformed all five of them into the same kind of bird, the Enchantress is not entirely sure that her magic is strong enough to transform them back into children. Transformation spells are complicated.

The Enchantress wears her own staff, when it is not in use, as a wooden ring around the second finger of her left hand. The other two she uses as crutches. Her magic has been demanding much of her strength; it is quite difficult to keep safe such a tally of individuals: her, the Huntsman, and the white mare that pulls the cart of blackbirds that were formerly children. She knows magic will only demand more from here. She sighs.

"Might I carry one of those for you?" the Huntsman says. He has a free hand. The other holds the reins of the horse, though the Enchantress suspects that this horse would go wherever the Huntsman tells it to go. She has seen the look in the mare's eyes. The horse has found a new master in him, and she will not let him from her sight.

"No," the Enchantress says. "I can carry them well enough myself." Her voice is clipped and unwelcoming. She does not want him to think that she needs his help. She is quite strong enough, quite efficient enough, on her own.

After a time, when they have walked several more miles, they stop by the side of a small water pool, where the horse drinks long and deep and the Enchantress kneels to fill a leather pouch of water. She must lay down the staffs in order to fill it. When she turns back from the water, she sees the Huntsman studying them.

"They are strangely different from one another," he says.

The Enchantress rises and studies the staffs with him. One has a gnarled knob at its top, and the wood that extends from the knob is twisted and curved in places that make it look as though it is a river. The other is completely straight, like a richly varnished walking stick, with a perfectly smooth ball at the top, on which is painted a golden dragon's eye.

"Every staff is different," the Enchantress says. "Shaped by its master."

"And yours," he says. He nods to the ring on her finger. "Yours is lovelier than any I have ever seen."

Her staff is a tall one with a slightly thick, pointed bottom, a thicker center that bends only slightly this way and then that—one bend of the river—and a rounded top that contains within it a small bit of sapphire.

The staff did not contain the sapphire until an old woman in the Weeping Woods of Fairendale gifted the Enchantress with a stronger, darker sort of magic. The Enchantress still does not fully understand this gift. It is a magic that enables her to transform children into blackbirds, balance several spells at the same time, and even heal small wounds, at seemingly no cost but a small energy expenditure. Or, perhaps a large one. Exhaustion sweeps over her.

The Enchantress does not answer the Huntsman. Instead, she says, "I grow weary of carrying these extra staffs. I have no power to Reduce them. Perhaps they would be just as safe resting in the cart next to the children." She holds them out for the Huntsman. "Would you kindly lay them inside?" She almost adds the word "gently," but the Huntsman is a clever man.

The Huntsman stares at the staffs and then up at the face of the Enchantress. He is surprised, and she understands. Little by little she has begun to trust him more, and she sees his pleasure scrawled plainly across his face. It is an uncomplicated trusting, however. There is no danger in handing the Huntsman these magical staffs. If he were a sorcerer—and he is not; there has never been a Huntsman with magic—he still could not use the staff of another. It has never been done. It is against the rules of magic.

The Huntsman smiles slightly and takes the first staff in his hands. A small spark flashes from his fingers. The Enchantress tilts her head. Another small spark flashes when he takes the second one.

The Huntsman, however, acts as though nothing unusual has happened. Was it her imagination, then? Did she see sparks of magic where none existed? Or is the Huntsman a magical man?

She dismisses this last question easily with a simple phrase: It has never been done.

She is merely tired. Her eyes have seen something that was not there.

The Enchantress presses her fingers to the sides of

her head, murmuring some words that will clear it effectively—a small Healing spell. But the muddle only thickens. The magic is growing stronger within her, while she grows weaker. It is because she expends so much strength to keep them safe.

In her darkest moments, tucked away in a tent that folds up to the size of a small speck of dust and is carried in her right shoe, the Enchantress thinks of all the magic she does every moment of every day. It is really quite astounding. There is not a minute that her magic is not touching the world. She keeps herself, the Huntsman, and the children perpetually Protected, which is highly uncommon among even the most skillful of sorcerers. No one is able to sustain a magical spell at all hours of every day, for as long as she has.

And in those darkest moments, several thoughts always slide into her mind: Will there be a limit? Will she reach her limit before they have finished their quest? Will she, at some point, be unable to protect them all from the dangers of these forests?

These thoughts keep her awake at night, but it is midday now, and she is uninterested in allowing them a foothold in the presence of the Huntsman.

The Huntsman has finished with the staffs. They rattle a bit in the cart as the white mare moves again. But they do not slide. He has arranged them to loop around the cages of their owners, though the Enchantress cannot fathom how he knows which bird is which child. She forgot as soon as she transformed the last one. There are too many now.

He is a Huntsman with a heart. She has never heard of such a thing. The stories tell of cruel and relentless Huntsmen, not those who care to know the names of their prey.

The Enchantress feels a prickling at the back of her neck. She turns around, but she sees nothing. She looks back at the Huntsman, who is staring in the same direction she had. This makes her shiver.

"Did you feel it?" he says.

"Yes," she says.

"There is something dangerous in this wood," he says.

"My magic will protect us," she says, though she falters slightly. She does not know if she can protect them from everything. There was, after all, a fairy ring that nearly killed the Huntsman and a serpent with poison that would have finished him if not for a mermaid who healed him.

Her legs weaken. She leans on her staff, which appears from practically nowhere. Perhaps they will have to slow their travel. But stretching out the travel, which will happen without her Hasten spell, will only put them in more danger. They are just outside the land of Rosehaven, in the northwestern part of the realm, and they must next journey to Lincastle, which is in the deep south. Without magic to speed them along, it would take them months to reach Lincastle.

She must use magic. The looking ball, which shows them all the lost children but, maddeningly, only one child at a time, seems to enjoy sending the Enchantress and the Huntsman back and forth and back and forth. Her Hasten spell is her retaliation for that inconvenience.

The Enchantress peers into the woods. Her chest tightens.

"Perhaps you should rest for a time," the Huntsman says. "Perhaps you should rest for a long while, in fact. You are quite pale."

The Enchantress looks up into his concerned face. Her eyes move to the cart and the five blackbirds that represent five of the lost children of Fairendale.

"I will watch over them," the Huntsman says. "You have nothing to fear."

"We must move on," the Enchantress says. "We must find the remaining children."

"But you are too weary," he says. "Your magic is

weakening you."

The urgency presses against her chest. "But we cannot slow our pace," she says. She cannot say, however, why it is that they cannot slow their pace. She cannot say that she fears what will happen when she has reached her limit, as she is fast doing. And they still have nineteen twelve-year-olds to find. Or, rather, eighteen. She knows where one of them is. She is only saving her until last.

"Well," the Huntsman says. "You could rest in the cart while I lead the way. I know how to find Lincastle. I know how to avoid Fairendale on our travels." His earnestness disarms her.

Still she shakes her head. "I cannot sleep while we travel," she says.

"Because you prepare our way," the Huntsman says.

"Yes," the Enchantress says.

"Perhaps we can try it for one day, then," the Huntsman says. "We shall not lose too much time in one day."

The Enchantress considers this. She considers his concern. She considers the weariness that persists though she rests and eats and rests. She considers the cart and the comfort of a traveling sleep. And, at last, she dips her head. "Very well, then," she says. "We will try it for one day and see how we progress."

"A day's rest will do wonders for you," the Huntsman says.

And the Enchantress can only hope.

He helps her to the cart. She summons a pillow from the speck of tent still lodged in her shoe as well as a thin sleeping mat made of soft feathers. She burrows beneath the fur that the Huntsman gave her, and the warmth encases her. The movement of the cart lulls her easily into sleep.

When she awakens, the trees have changed again. They are the broad and leafy trees of the Weeping Woods, tall and wide against a darkening sky. She sits up. "Fairendale," she says. Her voice stops the Huntsman.

"We have made good time," he says.

"How is it that we are in the land of Fairendale already?"

"We are not quite there," the Huntsman says. "These woods reach a long way. We have another day's travel before we will arrive on the perimeter of the land."

"But we have moved quickly," the Enchantress says. "While I slept."

"Perhaps your magic works even while you sleep," the Huntsman says. She cannot see his face, for he busies himself with the horse, allowing her to drink from a large leather skin that holds water. When he finishes tending the horse, he moves to the cart and puts his hand against its side. "I will find us some supper, and we will camp here for the night."

The clearing is much smaller than other clearings where they have camped. But it will do. "Supper would be nice," the Enchantress says. She has not eaten since early this morning.

But before the Huntsman can move away, a crack rings out through the woods. The Huntsman stills. He raises a finger to his lips. The white mare shifts, her ears pointed in front of her. The Huntsman faces that direction. The Enchantress feels her heart fluttering in her chest.

The Huntsman's voice is low when he speaks. "Something has been following us since we arrived in these woods," he says. "I did not want to wake you."

"What could it be?" she says.

"A sinister presence of some sort is all I know," he says. "I have been unable to find anything."

"Perhaps it does not want to be found," the Enchantress says. "Perhaps it wants to find us."

"I shall take care of it now," the Huntsman says, and he pulls a dagger from his boot. He steps slowly and carefully toward the woods. The Enchantress cannot bear to see him go.

"Huntsman," she says, and he startles but does not turn. "Leave it. We shall not be in these woods long. And even sinister presences cannot make it past my defenses."

The Huntsman looks back at her. He stares at her for a time, and then he replaces his dagger in his boot. "Very well, then," he says. "There is still the problem of supper."

"There is no problem," the Enchantress says. She feels stronger than she has in some time. She waves her staff in a small circle, and on the cart in front of her, two glass plates appear—one with a bit of bread and meat ringed in vegetables and the other with a large heap of leaves and a bit of oil dousing them.

"You must not use your magic where it is not required," the Huntsman says, and the Enchantress feels the sting of reproach.

"I am stronger now," she says.

"But you will spend your strength on what we can gather for ourselves," the Huntsman says.

"Only for this evening," she says. "Only to keep us safe."

The Huntsman relents and sits on the edge of the cart, eating the supper the Enchantress conjured from a bit of torn material that the Huntsman had bundled and put into the cart, saving for another day. She had teased him when he had done this, but she sees, now, that it was greatly needed. The heap is smaller, but it is not gone, and it will prove to be much more important than even the Huntsman thought at the time he gathered it.

They do not speak during the entire supper. The Huntsman continues to search the perimeter. The Enchantress watches him.

At last, when they have finished and the plates are empty of all leaves and meat and bread, she says, "Let us hope it is not the sort of presence that can break through the enchantments I have placed on this clearing."

"Let us hope," he says. He nods to the cart. "You sleep where you are. I will make my bed on the ground tonight."

The Enchantress does not thank him in words, but she thanks him with a thick pallet of the softest feathers and a large and fluffy pillow. His coat of many colors stretches across him, and she studies its brilliance until the fire dies out and the clearing goes dark.

It is Yasmin who watches the two of them in the small clearing. She intends fully to scare them, though she originally planned to do it with a terrifying shriek, not some silly stick resting on the forest floor. But the stick does just as well, and she figures she will have another chance, in the forthcoming days. She would like these two—and their magic; she can smell its power—to remain far from the kingdom of Fairendale; she has plans with which no one must interfere. Especially these.

She does not believe they are on her side. She sees far too much goodness in them both. It appeals to only a small, tiny portion of her.

They are powerful. But they have never met the likes of her, a woman handpicked by the Grim Reaper himself.

She laughs, and it crackles into the night, but, alas, the Enchantress and the Huntsman are already asleep and do not hear it except in their dreams.

Creatures draw near to her at the sound of her voice. She feels the power slide into her fingers. She locks eyes with two of the eight eyes that sit on the great head of a hairy spider. "You," she says. "You shall be called Spraiko."

Yasmin has been given the delicate task of naming the worst of the realm's creatures. She does not know why or how or from where she received this task. But it is in her hands, and she does it well and thoroughly. Thus far, on her travels, she has named many of the monsters that reside in the woods, monsters the people in our story do not even know exist. Take this spider, Spraiko, for example. He is monstrous, about one hundred times the size of a human, and he is not, unfortunately, the only one of his kind. He has a family, and by family I mean thousands of children tucked in a massive cave system just outside the lands of Morad. And his massive brother lives near Lincastle, with his own thousands of children.

Spraiko walks with silent steps and clicks pinchers at the front of his face—if it can, that is, be called a face—to communicate or express emotion or some other mysterious reason (even Yasmin does not know). Yasmin does know, however, that Spraiko is a spider that spins illusions in order to capture his prey and suck out their blood. He is quite good at what he does, and she knows this will be a great gift later.

But it is not yet time.

So she pats the giant spider, which is about the size of a large tank, on the head, which is bowed at the moment, and says, "It is not yet time, Spraiko. You will hear me when I call, and you will come."

And Spraiko clicks his pinchers together, as if in agreement, and scuttles away—if what he does can be called scuttling. It is more of a loping, a silent stepping, a fearsome sight of too many legs and joints and, it must be said, gigantic spider-like features.

Yasmin is not the least bit afraid, though I must confess: I would be.

She turns in the direction of Fairendale castle and begins her slow, graceful walk toward it.

Creature

The custom of the people of Lincastle, when one died, was to gather with candles and torches in the village streets at the close of the burial day. Those closest to the deceased stood in relative darkness, dependent on the light of the villagers to guide them through the streets and into the burial grounds that lay just east of the village, in a large, open field marked precisely for this purpose. As they walked in a long, winding procession, the people of the village sang. They sang songs that were melancholy and haunting, songs intended to usher the Grim Reaper and the spirits of the dead out of their village.

Any who witnessed the burial ritual would not soon forget it. Often, after a burial, the people of Lincastle heard those burial songs in their sleep and woke shivering, assessing the shadows in their rooms to make sure the Grim Reaper had not mistakenly arrived for them, too.

When the procession reached the burial ground, where the body would be lowered into the earth, the villagers stood in a circle around the hole that was dug earlier in the day by one of the village boys or girls assigned to the task. The ground around Lincastle was soft and pliable, which meant this job was not as difficult as it, perhaps, sounded. The people stood and sang. It was bad luck for all, they believed, to leave the grieving for a moment without song.

The body that waited to be buried this particular evening was not Gladys. Iddo, as was the custom, had wrapped a stiff and well-preserved body in a blue silken covering with white lace edging it. The body was so completely covered that no one would guess it was not Gladys. Only Iddo knew it was his wife's body, which he had preserved for two years and had, now, decided to let rest. So it was not without great emotion that Iddo stood that evening among the procession. This would be the first time Iddo would return to his work shop beneath the ground and not pass her body preserved in a glass case. It would be the first time that he would not look at her and say, "Soon, my dear. Soon we shall be together again."

He had needed a body. And he was not the sort of man to kill for his own purposes. So he had sacrificed. For the boy. For those who were still living.

Sebastien did not look at him throughout the burial ceremony. Perhaps he had hoped that Iddo would succeed before now. Iddo had hoped for that as well. But these things took time. Iddo had made some headway with the experiments. During one, the body had sat up for a moment in time, then collapsed back to the table. But it was something. It was progress.

Iddo watched some men of the village lower the body into the ground, and he felt a shuddering sob lodge in his throat. He pressed one hand against his mouth and gripped his staff with the other. The dirt thudded against the form as the hole filled. The people sang. Iddo closed his eyes.

"Goodbye, my love," he whispered.

A ship in the distance caught his eye. He had momentarily slipped in his attention and forgotten the enchantment this eve. He gripped his staff, recited the words in his mind, and felt the warmth pulse through him. The ship disappeared.

Iddo, though most did not know it, held only a small strain of magic, one given to him by his father when he was merely a boy. He was tasked with keeping the village of Lincastle—in fact, it was the entire realm of Fairendale, though the extent of this invisibility was not known—invisible to those who sailed the Violet Sea, which, in turn, kept those who sailed the sea invisible to the villagers. This was the only magic permitted him after becoming a father.

Were there those who sailed the Violet Sea? The stories of the land said that no one who sailed those waters would live to tell the tale. But that is not true. In fact, there are many who have sailed the Violet Sea, many who sail it still, who cannot, as desperately as they search, find their way back home.

The burial procession made its way back into the village streets and turned toward the home of Sebastien and Yerin. Iddo departed ways soon thereafter. There was, after all, work to do.

He stood in his workshop, looking at the empty glass case where his wife used to be. The light of life had dimmed in him. He felt it draining out, in a slow trickle as the grief of what he had done stole over him.

But there was work to do. He shuffled over to the body on the table and stroked the smooth forehead, which had turned a pale shade of blue. "You will wake soon," he said. He could not say why, but he felt sure of this.

He could not remember if he had locked the outer door to his work shop, so before beginning his work this evening, Iddo shuffled back along the dark passageway carved beneath the earth and climbed the uneven steps to the top. Yes. He had. He made his way back to the work shop, his hand trailing along the tunnel's sides, where roots and dirt clung to bits of rock. He left the passageway dark, for he did not want any to discover the secret outer door by light streaming through its cracks. He followed the light of the torches that cast his work room in a yellowish glow. He had built this tunnel and the attached workshop when his wife had died and his son had disappeared, when he felt the need to put his science to work on something that could erase sorrow. And he would erase sorrow, even if not his own.

The body of Gladys stared at him from the black iron table. The iron was cold when he touched it. The body was, too, but that would change, he knew.

If the machine did not work by tomorrow, Gladys would take the place of his wife's body in the glass case. It was the only preservation method Iddo had, and Gladys had already begun to decay. He smoothed down a patch of crumbling skin on her face. Perhaps he had waited too long for this part of the process. But he would not—he could not—give up now.

He worked on the machine unceasingly through that night and the following day. And when he was finished, he felt certain that it would work. He looked at the body, checked the straps that held it down, and then pulled the lever. Nothing happened. He cursed. He adjusted a few screws and knobs, and then he tried again. Nothing happened, except that the body's black hair became a twisted mass around her head, as though the shock of electricity had concentrated in her scalp. He cursed again. He adjusted more. He tried again. Nothing, except this time the smell of something burning reached his nostrils.

He walked over to the body and adjusted some of the suction-like cups attached to her face and her arms and her legs. He could not do much more to the body. Gladys did not look like Gladys any longer. The face had become gaunt and bony, as though the skin had melted and thinned a bit. The nose was particularly pointy, the cheekbones particularly sharp, the lips particularly nonexistent. She was a caricature of the woman she had been. Only her eyes remained the same, the black brows drawn up in what seemed like surprise. Iddo gave her lips a dash of red paint and dotted some pale pink, in circles, on her bluish cheeks. He did not know if it was better or worse.

He crossed the room to the lever. He checked all the knobs and twisted some dials. "One more time," he told himself. "And then I shall put the body away and rest for a while." He put his hand on the lever. He dropped his head, slumped his shoulders and said, "Please." He did not know to whom he was talking. Perhaps it was his missing father. He pulled the lever.

And it worked.

He had not really expected it to work, though he had hoped. But it was not magic. He did not think science could do something like this, when magic could not do it for most, either.

So it was with both horror and awe that he watched the body of Gladys slowly rise from the table. It lifted first its head, then its chest, then its entire upper half. It sat up and looked around in a slow, calculating way. Iddo felt a string of cold pull down his spine. What had he done? The thing before him was not a woman. It was a monster.

Its eyes locked with his. The eyes were dark, bottomless pits. The face twisted into a horrendous expression, something between a smile and a snarl. Iddo backed away, but the creature, still slowly and methodically, placed its feet on the ground of the work shop and stood. How had Gladys grown taller during the experiment? How had Iddo not noticed?

He remembered, suddenly, that this work shop was a secret one. No one knew he was here. No one would know whether he came out or remained within. His heart pounded, and the cold ran all along his arms and into his fingertips.

What had he done?

The creature's skin was patchy in places, as though it had decayed beyond repair. He would have to sew it together for her. But first he would have to convince her that he was her friend, her creator.

Her creator. The words shook him. He had never dreamed it would work.

Iddo spoke into the gathering silence. "I have brought you back to life." All thoughts of returning Gladys to her family vanished in that moment. He could not return this creature. It was far too monstrous. The boy and the man could not bear such a thing. Let them think she had been buried; the old Gladys *had* been buried, in all manner of the word. The creature before him was not Gladys. And this is what drew further words from Iddo's lips. "And I shall name you Yasmin."

The creature crossed the room in long, heavy steps. He did not think to run. He had created her, after all. Surely she would not turn on him.

But when the creature reached his side, she did not speak or do much of anything comforting at all. In fact, she held out a hand, which had somehow grown larger in the experimentation, and closed it around Iddo's throat.

He was a strong man. But even his strength struggled against the clutches of the creature called Yasmin, who was, once upon a time, a kind woman called Gladys. He thought he might die. He knew he would die. And just when he had closed his eyes and given himself over to the joy that would accompany seeing his wife and, perhaps, his son again, the creature dropped him and staggered toward the dark tunnel that led out into the world. Iddo, his weakness profound and all-consuming, crawled after her, desperate to keep her in and the world safe. If she had turned on her creator, what might she do to the others? And, perhaps more disturbing, what would she tell them? Would the village know what Iddo had done? It could not. The boy could not know. Yerin could not know. He had turned Gladys into a monster.

He did not, alas, reach her before she broke through the hidden door and lumbered out into the woods. By the time he himself reached the door, she was already gone.

Iddo stood looking, turning, staring and then stopping, trying to decipher some clue where the creature had gone. But there was nothing.

Risks

A knock sounds on Oscar's inn room door in the late afternoon. He is startled from dozing, a book open on his chest. When he opens the door, he sees Princess Freya.

She shoves into the room and glances behind her. She is breathing hard. "I came as soon as I could," she says.

"But we were not supposed to meet until tomorrow," Oscar says, questions hanging on his words. Has he slept so long? Is it already tomorrow?

"My mother urged me not to come," Princess Freya says. "But I had to."

Oscar shakes his head, perplexed, still not understanding why she is here.

"There is talk in the village," Princess Freya says. "The people are banding together, to capture the village children and hand them all over to the king of

Fairendale." Her eyes narrow. "Including me. Some men were storming into the castle as I fled. They intend to take me while my father is gone. Von Albeck…" She does not finish. Her jaw twitches. Fire blazes in her eyes.

"Why?" Oscar says. It is the only question he can think to ask.

Princess Freya shakes her head. "Some of the people here believe that only a man can rule a throne. And I am a girl." Her voice rises slightly on a tide of unspoken emotion.

Oscar would like to say so many things, but all that comes out is, "I will help you escape."

Princess Freya smiles at him. "I knew you would," she says. "I am not accustomed to running for my life. That is why I came here."

Oscar nearly tells her that he has never had to run for his life, either, but all the running comes back to him in flashes. The dashing into the Weeping Woods, the dragon lands, and then back through the Weeping Woods, to escape the king's men. He is more accustomed to this type of running than he would like to be.

"First," Oscar says, glancing around his room. He spots a change of his clothes, delivered here this morning. He tosses them at Princess Freya. "You must dress like a boy. They will never guess you are the princess."

She smiles at him, and he removes himself from the room, standing guard in front of the door. From downstairs, he can hear shouts and scuffles, and he knows that the people are here. Princess Freya throws open the door, and he has only a moment to take in her considerably changed appearance—she is a very pretty boy—before he says, "We will have to climb out a window." A look of fear flickers in her eyes for a moment, until he says, "I will go first. I will be waiting at the bottom to catch you if you slip."

She nods, and he pulls her toward the only window in the room, a small one that is just wide enough to fit his hips through. It is three stories down, but the stone side of the inn is uneven, which makes it easy to find his next step. When he has reached the bottom, he looks carefully around, but no one is in sight. He is behind the inn, closer to the woods, and this will be their advantage. Princess Freya looks at him from the window, her hair tucked neatly inside his black cap, and he nods. He can hear the din of people inside the inn. Her progress is painstakingly slow, and when he hears the door above them burst open, he says, "Let go!" and Princess Freya does. She falls toward him, and he catches her but loses his balance. They roll and then are on their feet, running toward the woods as though they never lost a step.

Oscar feels a heavy sense of having done all of this before. His feet slow, but Princess Freya drags him on.

They reach the woods and continue running until they are deep inside. Only then do they stop, their chests heaving.

"You flew," Oscar says between breaths.

"We will have to work on the landing," Princess Freya says. They laugh, but their voices are subdued, quiet. Oscar looks around. They are so deep in the woods that the sunlight hardly reaches them. And then he realizes that the sun is not in the sky anymore. It has set. They have run for a long time.

"Perhaps we should find a place to rest for the night," he says.

"We must keep moving," Princess Freya says. "I do not think the people of Lincastle give up so very easily, especially when money is involved."

Oscar shakes his head. "They have enough money," he says.

"They do not believe so," Princess Freya says. "They believe they need more."

"They do not know what it means to need more," Oscar says.

"Perhaps," Princess Freya says. "We all have our vices."

"And yours is excusing others for their greed and obsessions," Oscar says, unable to stop the words from burning through his lips.

Princes Freya looks at him, her eyes sad. "No," she says. "I only know that there is more to every story. And if we are not interested in looking for it, well, then we are no better than they are."

Oscar turns away. And only then does he see the man with shining eyes, staring at them with a dangerous smile on his face. Oscar gasps.

It is the bookseller.

"I knew I would find you," the bookseller says. "I knew I would make you pay."

"You will do nothing of the sort," Princess Freya says.

The bookseller seems startled to hear a girl's voice coming from a boy. He looks her up and down, squints his eyes, moves slightly closer. "Princess?" he says.

"Yes," Princess Freya says. She takes off Oscar's cap and shakes out her dark hair. "I am protecting Oscar from the likes of you."

"The rules do not apply out here in the woods," the bookseller says, his grin growing. "No one will ever know. The both of you will fetch a pretty coin." And with that, he clicks his tongue, and a black horse moves out from the shadows, pulling a small cart. "Now then," the bookseller says. "Who wants to come first?" He smiles with his yellow, crooked teeth.

Oscar and Princess Freya both struggle valiantly, but in the end, it is their protective impulse that seals their fate. Rather than run, they remain, trying to save each other from the bookseller and his ropes. But they cannot.

He ties them up like animals, pulls cloths over their eyes, and orders the horse to move. The cart jerks forward, vibrating Oscar's teeth.

He has never wished more than this moment that he was born with the gift of magic.

Maude stares out the window in the sitting room of the Enchantress's cottage, where she has been both patiently and impatiently—a paradox that is easy to understand when one is both excitedly anticipating something and yet humbly attempting to wait without complaint—awaiting her daughter's return to life. Not that Hazel is dead, exactly. She is merely hanging in the balance between life and death. Maude, of course, would rather she come back to life than slip silently into death, but the only power she has over the situation is the power of waiting. She has waited for so many days. For so many days she has longed for something to change. And today, something has.

Outside the window, the shoe-shaped house, where Maude lived for a time with twenty-two of the lost children of Fairendale, has begun to flicker into view. This is slightly alarming, because the house was under a very complicated enchantment wherein it would remain invisible to any who might pass it in the woods. Maude is not entirely certain that this bit of change should be alarming; she does not know if others can see it. But Maude is a natural worrier, and she only knows that yesterday she could not see it and today she can. Something is amiss.

She longs to return to that house and its warmth and familiarity, though she did not live there long. She has been so lonely of late. Waiting. Always waiting. Will she never be done with waiting?

But she will wait as long as she must to see her daughter wake. She will remain vigilant, at her side, protecting her from whatever may come her way.

What really disturbs Maude about the shoe-shaped house's sudden visibility is that she fears it means the house of the Enchantress, where she and Hazel are, has also become suddenly visible. If the enchantment protecting this house has been weakened or, worse, removed, will she, a woman without the gift of magic, be able to fend off what might come for her daughter?

Will something come for her daughter?

She really should have agreed to the trip Arthur planned long ago, when Hazel and Theo were still young: a trip to restore her magic and Arthur's as well. Magic would be a great help in times like these. Maude has been feeling a heavy sense of dread for some time now, and it trails its freezing fingers up her back and over her shoulders and into her chest. Something will come for her daughter; it is a certainty in her mind. She does not have Arthur here to talk her out of her bend toward pessimism.

Maude shivers. If only the Enchantress would return. Where is she? Where are the lost children? Where is Arthur, her husband; Theo, her son; the people of Fairendale, whom she once called friends?

Maude walks in and out of the cottage's rooms on restless legs, back and forth, back and forth, back and forth. She bends over Hazel and whispers, "Wake up, daughter," knowing full well that her simple words will not rouse the girl. She walks into the room of the Enchantress and touches the bed and the silks hanging in the wardrobe and the golden brush sitting on a dresser. She paces out to the kitchen and sets a pot on to boil. A bit of soup will do her good, perhaps.

And while she is waiting—still waiting—she presses her forehead to the pane of the small window in the kitchen and stares out at the shoe-shaped house. And while she is staring, something shifts. Something larger and dark. A cloud of some sort, resting over the house. Maude squints her eyes. It curls and bends and reaches fingers into the windows. It is searching for something. It is peeling back the layers of invisibility. It is invading.

And then it is gone, and Maude has a sudden brilliant idea. She can see the garden now. It is still, miraculously, as vibrant as it ever was. While the storehouse of the Enchantress never seems to run dry, as though there is some kind of enchantment that replenishes every bit of food Maude takes from it, the Enchantress also does not keep many of Maude's favorite vegetables in her storehouse—squash and cabbage and peppers. She can see the red of the peppers from here. She tilts her head. Perhaps she can take some and bring them back here, so long as she is quick about it.

She ventures out to the porch. Her foot clicks on the first step. She descends carefully, watching for the dark gray cloud. It does not return. So she runs, as fast as she has ever been able to run, and skids to a stop in the garden. She takes whatever she can gather, lifting her apron in a fold and stuffing the vegetables inside it. She stuffs so many that some of them roll out the sides, but it does not matter. She is nearly finished. She turns.

And what she sees when she turns steals her breath from her chest. She gives a cry of alarm, though there is no living person in these woods who can hear her.

All around her are people but not people at all. They are graying people, flickering people, there one moment and gone the next and quickly back again. They flicker and fade and steadily draw closer, as though they are one and the same force, pulled along in a tightening band around her. Maude turns around and around and around, and there is, alas, no escape.

They stop as one, near her, but not near enough to touch. And then one walks through their ranks, his steps measured, his black robe flapping wildly in a wind that Maude cannot feel on her face, so frozen is it in fear and anguish and regret.

His silver scythe gleams like an upside-down smile.

The Grim Reaper is out in broad daylight. This is an overstep of his former powers, but, fortunately, he has grown quite strong, and the land of Fairendale has also grown quite dark. He is no longer bound to darkness and shadow; he can now move about freely, day or night. So he has, today, taken his opportunity.

The woman stands before him. There is no one who can stop him now. He will finally claim one of the magical people he deserves.

And with her powers, he will collect on all the ones who have cheated their deaths and weakened him in this game.

He lifts his scythe in the air, and the Black Eyed Beings close in.

Cora turns over a talisman in her hands. It is a bronze talisman, and carved into it is the image of a blackbird resting on a blooming branch. This talisman hung about the neck of the prince before she transformed him into a blackbird—some sort of protective charm. She can feel the magic thrumming through it. She strokes the bronze.

She has a talisman like it, only it bears a carved blackbird with its head tilted. There is no blooming branch.

Perhaps the blooming branch is the secret of the

magic in the prince's talisman. Cora does not know for certain.

Today, she has tried to use the magical talisman to return the prince to his former state—that of a boy, not a blackbird. She has tried three times, and three times she has failed.

What has happened to her magic? Does she still possess the gift? The thought that her magic is gone, forever, infuriates her. It is the dragon's fault. She did not intend, when she visited the dragons of Morad, to become a dragon rider, but that is precisely what happened. It was most unexpected and most unwanted. Is this what has stolen her magic?

She has searched her extensive collection of books for information about what happens when a rider finds her dragon, and she has read nothing at all about riders or even dragons. It is as though when King Sebastien took over the throne, when he banished the dragons from the kingdom of Fairendale, he banished, too, every book that contained some information about the creatures of old.

Cora has not asked the village book seller. She has been unable to face the village people, after Sir Greyson told them she was responsible for the former king's death.

She is still cross with him about this, but she misses him terribly. The loneliness is a pulsing ache in her chest.

Cora shoves it away.

Something of use might remain in the castle library, but Cora would rather go to the source. Which is what she plans to do.

Cora stands. She pats the blackbird on the head and sets the talisman on the windowsill, where the blackbird prefers to sit, though the window does not look out on anything but earth; the room in which the prince, as a blackbird, is kept is underground and, conveniently, invisible to those who are not chosen to see it. "I am sorry, Prince," Cora says. "Something has interrupted my powers, and I must reawaken them. And as soon as I do, you will be, once more, a boy."

The blackbird twitters.

Cora slides through the secret passageway beneath the Fairendale fountains and stands gazing out across the dying land. No one has magic enough to restore what has been lost, but she tried occasionally—a flower lifted here, a patch of grass greened there. She used to hide her powers in fear that someone would mark her a dark sorceress, which she supposes she is; it is only dark magic that remains in a sorcerer or sorceress after one has children. Cora does not bother with propriety now. The land of Fairendale needs her magic. Which infuriates her further. Her magic is needed and yet it is gone.

She twists into a blackbird with a flash of feathers and wings her way to the dragon lands faster than her feet would carry her. Miles and miles she goes, and she is not the least bit weary when she lands.

She is, however, slightly chilled. The land has grown colder in the days since the children disappeared, and it will not cease growing colder, she fears, until they are returned, safe and sound. She does not understand this magic, but she perceives it: the land of Fairendale is bound to its children.

Cora attempts to cloak herself in a Concealment spell (*Let it work*, her heart says) and lifts her hands at the boundary of Morad. She is not foolish enough to cross it. She waits for the dragon's approach but does not open her eyes. She is not afraid; the one thing she does know about dragons and their riders is that they are bound life to life. What happens to her happens to him. If he harms her, he, too, will be harmed. It is an ancient piece of magic that happens spontaneously and automatically and cannot be summoned except by using the darkest and strongest magic. She has never attempted the summoning of this spell herself, though it might be useful someday.

The problem with the darkest and strongest magic is that playing with it is dangerous. The darker and stronger the magic, the more a sorceress must pour in parts of herself, to retain control, thus risking those parts being lost forever and the dark parts of magic filling the missing holes. Stories tell of many dark sorcerers and sorceresses to whom this very thing happened, and they were never, ever the same. It was a warning every magical child heard at the start of their studies. A sorceress must not lose herself, for it is only in full possession of self—which is the definition of light magic—that dark magic, when used for ill gain, can be destroyed.

And where are the stories, Cora wonders, that tell of a land bound to the presence of children? This must be the case for Fairendale. The land dies without its children, though its village people and royal rulers remain. No land has ever seen the vanishing of its sun, and this very thing happened in Fairendale the day the children departed. Only brief glimpses of the sun are permitted now.

Cora feels the ground shake beneath her and knows the dragon is on his way. His breath is hot on her face, and it is not until she can feel its wind that she opens her eyes and sees his blazing red ones, flecked with black pebbles.

"You desecrate this land again," the dragon hisses at her. The gray underside of his neck reddens, as though the fire within him is aching to burst free.

Cora tilts her head, a tremor gripping her chest. But she will not let him see that she is afraid. "I have not entered your land," she says.

"I do not want you here," Blindell says.

"I do not want to be here," Cora says. She waits for a moment, letting the words sink in. And then she says, "I do not want this any more than you do."

The dragon growls, but the sound is somewhat softer.

"I have come to find out what you know about dragons and riders," Cora says. "Perhaps we might reverse what has been done, with a bit of magic."

"I will tell you nothing," Blindell says, but then, as if contradicting his own angry words, he continues. "There is no reversal of what has been done."

"Well," Cora says. "That is unfortunate."

"You should not have touched me," Blindell says. "It would never have happened."

"I have heard differently," Cora says. "I have heard that a dragon will find his rider regardless of what one or the other does. This Life for Life Bond is a gift, the stories say, and it lies in the hands of magic, not a dragon or a person."

"I do not want my life bound to yours," Blindell says.

"And yet it is," Cora says.

The dragon hisses, a flame erupting from his mouth.

It singes a tree beside her. "You have come to find out more about dragons and riders," Blindell says. His eyes flash. "And yet you know so much."

"Only what I have heard in stories," Cora says. "But I suspect you know more."

The dragon stares at her for a moment, and then he lowers his head so that it is even with her eyes. "What is it you wish to know?" he says.

Cora weighs her words before she speaks. "Tell me, does a rider lose her gift of magic if she is bonded with a dragon for life?"

She can see that her question has surprised Blindell, for his eyes flicker momentarily with a light, orangish-red. "I have never heard of such a thing," he finally says.

"Good," she says. "Then it is not you who has stolen my magic. Perhaps it is someone else."

"And yet you are invisible," he says. He looks back at the dragons that lie in varying positions on the sands of Morad. None of them turn his way. Cora gazes along with him.

"Yes," she says. "I suppose I am." She looks down at her hands, at the staff that rests against the ground. She looks up and around. She has conjured a Concealment spell, this is true. But is it only in the presence of the dragon that she is permitted use of her gift?

Well, she will have to bring the prince to the dragon. But first she will have to determine whether this would be safe. She knows Blindell throbs with the need for revenge. If the prince were in front of him, he might not be able to resist.

So she says, "I have the prince," and she lets the words hang between them.

Blindell's eyes flash their customary deep red. "You have the prince?" he says.

"Yes," she says.

"I demand that you bring him to me," Blindell says.

"So that you might kill him?" Cora says.

"As my father and mother were killed by his grandfather," Blindell says.

"He is not his grandfather," Cora says. "I believe you desire revenge on King Sebastien, who never cared for anyone but himself. And now he is dead." She does not add that she was responsible for his death all those years ago.

Blindell lets loose a long and rumbling roar. Cora lifts the staff and the hand that does not hold it, catches the sound in her arms, and presses it beneath the ground. "You do not want the others to hear," she says.

"You will bring the prince to me," Blindell says.

"We will come to an agreement," Cora says. "I will

bring the prince to you, but you must not hurt the boy."

"You will bring the boy to me, and I will do as I please," Blindell says.

"That is not how agreements work," Cora says.

"There is no agreement," Blindell hisses.

"But there must be," Cora says. "I will not bring the prince without an agreement."

"Then I will rain fire over every home in the village, and the castle, too," Blindell says. He draws himself up to his full height. Cora must look up into the sky to see him.

"Not if I protect it," Cora says, though she knows her magic does not work in the village.

"Your magic has been stolen," Blindell says, and Cora's heart turns cold for a moment. She was foolish to let the words slip. She searches for others, and she finds them.

"I can feel it returning even now," she says.

"You do not have magic enough to protect a village from me," Blindell says.

Cora laughs, though she is quaking inside. "Oh, but I do," she says. "And I will."

"Bring the prince to me," Blindell says, this time in a low and measured voice that is much more frightening than his roaring one.

Cora stares at him for a moment. She tilts her head

and says, "No," and at the very moment she utters the word, she flashes back into a blackbird. Blindell strikes with sound and fury, crashing through the forest, lunging for her, taking to the sky, flapping for a moment and cracking his terrible teeth together. One of those teeth nicks a leg, before Cora is fully blackbird, but she escapes with her life.

She looks back once, to see a path blazed through the forest. If she were not currently a blackbird, she would smile. That destruction will get him in trouble with the dragons, and perhaps he will be much more accommodating when next she visits.

Halfway across the Weeping Woods, Cora is struck by such an icy blast of dread that she hovers in place. She looks through her blackbird eyes, all through the forest to see what she can see. But she sees nothing. She only feels it, a danger of an entirely different sort, on its way to Fairendale.

Cora emerges from the woods in her human skin, blood dripping from her right leg, where the dragon's teeth grazed her. It is deep and will need tending. She attempts a Healing spell, but it does not work. She clenches her teeth and straightens. She breathes the stagnant air of Fairendale's land. No more sweet scent of flowers. No more comforting feel of green grass beneath her bare feet. No more sheep bleating in the fields beyond. It is no longer the home she has loved all her life. And it may be some time before it will become that home again.

But it will. Of this she is quite certain. And she will persist until Fairendale is restored to its former beauty.

We last left Arthur and Zorag face to face with a fearsome dragon leader and his first in command, and now, I am afraid to tell you, we return to him in a much more dire state. If one were to look across the land of Gyria, as Arthur does now, even the most unobservant would notice that there are no longer any Fire Mountains cutting the horizon. There are only dragons circling Arthur and Zorag.

Arthur thinks only one thing: Zorag was right. There are no Fire Mountains. There are only dragons—which means the people of Ashvale vanished in a dragon attack, not an eruption. This knowledge shocks him. Had the people of Ashvale known? Had they seen the dragons in their last moments?

The ground trembles. The largest dragon—the one Arthur assumes is the leader—speaks. "Leave our land," he says, "if you would like to live."

"Kaleed," Zorag says. "Please. Listen."

Arthur looks at Zorag, confused. Does Zorag know this leader? Has he once again kept information from Arthur as he did when they visited the land of Eyre, which was ruled by Zorag's uncle?

"Leave our land," the dragon says again, "if you would like to live."

Zorag drops his head to the ground. He does not lift his eyes, but he says, "I am Zorag of Morad."

Kaleed roars, and Arthur must grab Zorag to keep from falling again. But then the copper dragon quiets, and after a moment of the most terrifying silence imaginable, Kaleed says, "Zorag, you say?"

"Yes," Zorag says. "I am he."

"The king of Morad?" Kaleed says. "Ruler of the realm?"

"It is me," Zorag says. He still does not lift his head.

Kaleed drops his wings slightly. Zorag remains as he is. "Tell me," Kaleed says. His voice is rough and wary. "Why are you here?"

"We have come for your help," Zorag says, eyes fixed on the ground.

The dragons roar around him, and Arthur watches, horrified and yet unable to look away. Will they erupt like

Fire Mountains, right here? Kaleed hisses, and the dragons quiet.

"And why would we help you?" Kaleed says. "You have nothing we need."

"You do not need me," Zorag says. "But I need you."

"Well, well. You need us," Kaleed says. "And what will you do for the dragons of Gyria? What has the king of Morad ever done for the dragons of Gyria?" One of Kaleed's two primary eyes blazes with a green glow so fierce that Arthur cannot stand the brilliance. He must look away. Zorag closes his eyes and shakes his head, still not lifting his face to the dragon.

"I have done nothing," Zorag says. "And I regret it every day."

"You regret it when you need something," Kaleed says, and because the hurt that wrings out his voice is so surprising, Arthur fastens his eyes on the dragon's copper face for a moment. Then he looks at Zorag. Then back. Zorag to Kaleed to Zorag. Has he missed something?

A long slash cuts across the other primary eye on Kaleed's face, the one that does not glow. All the dragon's small eyes are closed, but this one puffs open in a pucker of skin and scar.

"Get out of my kingdom," Kaleed says.

"But the realm will fall," Zorag says.

"Do I care for the realm?" Kaleed says. "Am I the ruler of the realm?"

"How the realm goes is how Gyria goes," Zorag says. "You should care about that."

The dragons that encircle them hiss, their tongues flickering out along with a bit of red liquid that dances at the forked end. Arthur huddles behind Zorag, but there is nowhere he can go to escape what appears to be all-consuming rage and hate.

Kaleed, however, hushes his dragons. He does not say anything when they are quiet, but Zorag fills the space. "The other kingdoms will fall," Zorag says. "Because of what passes in Fairendale."

"Fairendale," Kaleed says. The word is soaked in derision and disgust. Arthur feels it spear into the center of his chest. "I never understood why you dragons of Morad loved that land."

"We did not love the land," Zorag says. "We loved its people."

The two dragons stare at one another for several moments. Arthur, whose hand is still resting against Zorag's leg, feels the dragon's heart beat once, twice, three times before Zorag speaks again. And when he speaks, his voice is gentle yet strong. "It was not your fault. You did not have the proper information. And you are forgiven."

Kaleed lifts his face into the sky, his horns pointed toward the ruined land of Ashvale, and roars long and loud and unstoppable. When he is finished, all the dragons of Gyria drop their heads. Arthur does the same. He does not think he can bear to look in the eyes of this dragon king and see what regret is held within them.

"I am gathering a dragon army," Zorag says softly.

The copper dragons of Gyria shift, a hissing sound rising on the air again. "And you think that the dragons of Gyria would willingly join your army?" Kaleed says, his voice slightly barbed, slightly muted. "You could demand our allegiance, and we would be bound to you. A command would be more effective than a request."

Zorag's head drops. "I am only on a quest to ask help from all the dragons." His voice is low, humble, deeply sad. "I would never require it."

"What will the dragons gain should they help?" Kaleed says.

"Freedom," Zorag says, without hesitation.

"We have freedom enough already," Kaleed says. "Do you see any people in our land?" His voice hitches slightly.

"No," Zorag says. He pauses, starts, stops, starts again. "We shall leave you to your freedom, then." His eye catches Arthur's, and Arthur knows it is time to climb on his back. He glances at the dragons and moves toward Zorag's left rear leg. But the voice of Kaleed stops him.

"And what other dragons have joined you?" Kaleed says.

"None as yet," Zorag says.

"We are the first you have asked?" Kaleed says. His voice softens slightly, though still rough and rusted around the edges.

"No," Zorag says. "I flew to my uncle first."

"Ah," Kaleed says. "And how fares Rezedron? We heard he is ill."

"He is dying," Zorag says. He lifts his head now. "He cannot help."

"And neither can we," Kaleed says. He once again assumes his tallest position, which makes his long neck appear to be a question mark. Arthur tilts his head and opens his mouth, but before he can squeeze the words out of the tight band of his throat, Zorag pushes him behind a leg.

"Very well," Zorag says. "We will continue our quest alone."

"Leave our land," Kaleed says. "And do not come back. Ever."

Zorag drops his head again. "It was good to see you,

old friend," he says. Arthur climbs onto his back, and Zorag lifts into the sky, his damaged wing causing him to falter momentarily, which causes Arthur to slip slightly and dig his fingernails into the scales, which causes Zorag to cry out with a long and mournful roar. Or perhaps he cries out for the whole and heavy disappointment, frustration, anger, sadness he feels upon visiting two dragon lands and being no closer to building a dragon army than he was before. It is certainly heavy enough to draw tears from Arthur as well.

Arthur rests his head against the dragon's back and listens to the whooshing rhythm of beating wings.

Waiting

Iddo heard the reports the following day. The people of Lincastle believed there was a monster living in the woods surrounding the village. This, of course, was a different monster than all the others that had been sighted throughout the years, the ones that kept the people of Lincastle practically imprisoned within their open land. This one, they said, had bluish skin, ghastly red lips, and pink circles on its cheeks. Its hair, they said, was wild and black, like a dark cloud following it wherever it went. The creature, they said, growled, hissed, and lunged; it ventured into the streets of the village as no other creature had ever done.

Iddo cringed.

The people, as often happens when a threat of this kind becomes more personal, began to talk of forming a search party—perhaps a better term for this party was an execution party.

Iddo cringed still more.

And, if that were not enough, the villagers began to point fingers, blaming one another for bringing a monster to the village. Their neighbor was too greedy, they said. Their neighbor was too sullen, they said. Their neighbor was too selfish, they said. Riots raged in the streets. People cursed at one another. The entire community was falling apart.

Iddo cringed until he knew he must move.

For a fleeting moment, he considered appealing to Yerin and Sebastien. He thought, somewhat irrationally, that their help might calm the monster, if she recognized them. But, in the end, he decided it was too great a risk— for both himself and the boy. He did not care much for Yerin, but he would not have the creature he had made kill the boy he had grown to love.

One night, Iddo tracked the beast deep into the woods. He found her wrapping her arms around a tree, about to pull it from its place in the ground. He tilted his head. Why would Yasmin want to pull a tree from the ground?

"Yasmin," he said. The creature turned around snarling. Her eyes had a wild and feral look about them.

He took a step back, hardly noticing he moved. She was a fearsome creature indeed, and her days in the forest, of which there had been several, had knotted up her black hair and rendered her even more fearsome. Her blue skin had peeled away in more places, leaving gray patches on the skin of her arms. But Iddo could see, still, a vestige of humanity buried beneath the monster. And so he thought, perhaps irrationally again, that he could tame her.

"I must take you home," Iddo said. He held out his hand. "If you would come."

The creature did not say anything. Perhaps she did not know how to speak. She merely stared at him with those wild, empty eyes. Iddo took one infinitesimal step forward, his muscles tensed and ready for flight.

"Would you like to see your family?" he said. Yasmin tilted her head, but the look she gave him only sent another shiver dashing down his back. Should he run? Should he continue appealing to the small scrap of humanity that remained within her? He did not know.

And then the creature spoke. "My family," she said. Her voice creaked out from her lips and dissipated in the warm, heavy air. Iddo was amazed. The creature could speak. Yasmin could speak!

"Yes," he said. "Do you know what a family is?"

Yasmin's eyes narrowed to slits. "Of course I know what a family is," she said. "What do you think I am?"

He did not answer this question, of course, for she would not like to know what he thought she was. But he could see, now, that she was more than simply a beast.

"You do not fear me?" Yasmin said. Iddo, quite by accident, had an interesting revelation: all her lunging and hissing and growling at the people had been only a defense against the way they had feared her. All she had wanted was their love.

He knew this because he knew what he, himself, wanted.

"No," Iddo said, and he meant the words.

"You created me," she said. "Why?"

"To return to your family," he said.

"I cannot return like this," she said. She looked at her arms and down at the ground.

"No," Iddo said. "You cannot. But perhaps I might help."

Her eyes lifted to his, and for a moment he saw hope within them. They brightened considerably, and then, quite as suddenly, they dimmed once again. "You should have let me die," she said. Her eyes turned hard and vicious. "Now he will not take me back."

Iddo cleared his throat. He remembered, in that

moment, that she was a powerful being—stronger and faster and larger than he was. If she turned angry… well, he did not want to think about what might possibly happen.

"He?" Iddo said, for want of anything better.

"I must do something for him before he will take me back," Yasmin said. She turned from Iddo and wrapped her arms around the tree before her.

"Wait!" Iddo said, his voice ringing out and reverberating through the woods. The trees in the land of Lincastle were sacred. A curse came upon any who harmed one of them. This was part of the folklore of the land, passed down to every man, woman, and child, to ensure that the people remained well protected from the dangers of the sea and forest creatures—to ensure, more specifically, that Lincastle remained hidden and well protected from invaders, should any exist.

"I must rid the forest of its living trees," Yasmin said. "This is the task the Grim Reaper has given me."

"But I am your creator," Iddo said, hoping. "And I command you to stop."

Yasmin whirled around, her purple dress a blurred frenzy around her legs. "You are nothing to me," she said.

Iddo felt another prick of fear. But he had,

fortunately, come prepared. He unlatched the sword he had hidden, somewhat awkwardly, inside his breeches and took a dagger from his boot. He had, once upon a time, learned to fight like a master swordsman, and even if he lacked the strength, at least he had the weapons. And these weapons were doused with a sleeping potion. So if, in the struggle, he managed to connect one of the tips with any part of Yasmin's skin, she would sleep. He would not have to kill her, and he would also not have to die.

Yasmin smiled a wicked smile. Her teeth gleamed in the gathering darkness. "The Grim Reaper will not like that you have taken such a person as me from him," she said, by way of warning. Another cold breath shivered down Iddo's back. "He is waiting to see which of us will die. Right over there." Iddo, in a moment of folly, followed the arc of her arm and the point of her finger, to a shadowed corner of the woods. He saw nothing before Yasmin was upon him. He did not even have a moment to consider what his fear was shouting in his head: *Run.*

He did not run; even if he was not locked in Yasmin's grip, which he was, he would not have run. He had to finish this.

Yasmin knocked him to the ground, and his hands

lost their grip on both his weapons. Her hands went around his neck, and he felt the breath ram against his throat and pitch back down into his stomach. It had nowhere else to go. He patted the ground around him. Where was his dagger? Where was his sword? Where was the strength that he had felt only moments ago? It was as though Yasmin could drain him of life simply by touching him. His fingers felt something cold and metal. He reached, reached, reached, and finally grasped a hilt in sweaty palms, instantly dropped it, then picked it up again. Yasmin's knee slammed against his hand. He cried out but made no sound at all, for he had little breath remaining. Her knee pinned his hand flat, and he could no longer move. So he would die, then. Well, he had lived a good life. He had tried, at the very least.

But, most unexpectedly, Yasmin collapsed on top of him, a heavy, sleeping weight. Iddo rolled her off, and her body, limp, thumped the ground beside him. He gasped, choked, clawed for air. Beside him, Yasmin's eyes were closed, her face composed in what could almost be called a lovely, serene expression. Almost. The point of his dagger was lodged in her shoe. It must have punctured her foot.

Iddo laughed, more from relief than anything else. He lay back down for a moment, breathing, enjoying the feel of air moving through his lungs. When he had properly marveled at the magnificence of being alive, he sat up and looked around. The eyes of the forest watched him. Even he did not know all the creatures living here. His cottage, which was not so very far away, was enchanted like all prophets' cottages, to keep it safe from the dangers of the forests. Prophets most often lived in the woods; they needed space and quiet to See their Visions.

It was growing dark. Iddo would have to hurry.

He gathered Yasmin in his arms, and though his legs were weak and tired, he ran through the trees, stumbling over rocks and roots, never glancing behind him. He left his sword and dagger where they lay and hoped that he would have no need of weapons on his swift flight home.

And he made it. Barely. A creature thudded into the protective shield that had been in place around his cottage for centuries. Iddo did not even look to see what the creature looked like. He had nightmares enough as it was.

He took Yasmin down beneath the ground, through the tunnel and into his secret workshop. Inside, he had arranged heavy iron chains of the old-fashioned kind: bracelets and chain links connected to a large ball. He had acquired them from the village mason. Each chain had required no less than ten men to lift them from the delivery cart and transfer them to the four sturdy wagons Iddo had arranged in his garden. As soon as the men departed, Iddo had rolled the chains, wagon by wagon, down the secret stairs (he used a long slab of wood to smooth the stairs and minimize capsizing, since he did not think he would be able to right an overturned wagon on his own), through the secret passage, and into the secret room, and then he had collapsed for the rest of that day.

Now they would be used as they were intended. He laid Yasmin on the dirt floor, propped up against the wall. Her head lolled forward, but her eyes did not open. With great effort, Iddo lifted one iron bracelet and snapped it around Yasmin's right wrist. He lifted another and snapped it around her left wrist. He rolled the two remaining to her feet and secured them to her ankles.

He stood back and crossed his arms.

"Now," he said, though Yasmin had not yet woken. "I will fix your skin and you will do as I say."

He got to work. He patched her skin in places, securing, with thick black stitches, pieces of flesh he had stored in jars (he had a great many jars with a great many things; he was a scientist, after all) to what remained of her own bluish-tinted skin. She did not need any on her face, though her arms and legs required much work.

He brushed her with a preservation liquid that smelled of strong chemicals, then spritzed her with rose water.

When he was finished, he moved to the other side of the room and waited for her to wake.

The first thing she did was look around. Then she growled. Then she said, "Why am I here?"

"I am sure you will understand," Iddo said. Her head jerked toward him, and her chains rattled, but she could go nowhere.

She growled again, but this time it ended in what sounded like a cry of anguish. "I must have the light," she finished. "I must."

"I will bring you light," Iddo said. "But you cannot go outdoors. The people cannot know you are here. You must remain a secret. I must remain a prophet."

"The Grim Reaper will find you," Yasmin said. "He will make you pay for what you have done." Her eyes did not appear nearly as angry as her words. They held mostly sadness. She hung her head.

Night and day, Iddo kept the torches blazing in the underground room. Yasmin remained in chains, but Iddo brought her water and food from his own table. In fact, sometimes he would dine with her; he was a lonely man.

Occasionally, Yasmin would ask if Iddo ever intended to let her go.

"That depends on you," he would say.

For a time, when he answered this way, the chains would rattle as if she were trying to get away by her own strength. But one day they stopped rattling, and her head hung ever after.

When this happened, Iddo began to bring her books from his father's library, still hoping that one day she would be all that he wanted her to be.

So Yasmin remained, bound and hidden, in a secret work shop behind Iddo's cottage. So Iddo remained, hoping, always hoping.

And so, too, did the Grim Reaper remain, watching the two, waiting.

Surprises

It takes Iddo, the prophet who once trained King Sebastien in the dark arts of magic and who also became the keeper of the monster Yasmin when he created her out of a scientific experiment gone wrong, quite some time to realize that Yasmin is missing. He is ashamed to admit this. Because of the thick and arduous weight of guilt—guilt for attempting such a foolish experiment, guilt for taking an innocent human being and turning her into a monster, guilt for his unforgivable failure—Iddo had taken to leaving food for Yasmin just outside the door where she was imprisoned. The chains that held her had grown longer over the years and allowed a bit of freedom, at least within the room, which had nothing in it but stone walls. He could not have her attempting escape, after all. He had to deprive her of anything and

185

everything, for escape would mean danger to many.

This, at least, is what he told himself.

In the beginning, Iddo had often sat with her, attempting to humanize her. When that did not work, he left her books as a consolation to company. Once he even mistakenly left her a portion of the Old Man's Great Book. All he had was a portion. The copy that had belonged to Folen, Iddo's father, had disappeared long ago. At the time, Folen had replicated a portion of the book by his own hand and with his own remarkable memory. It ended abruptly, right in the middle of a Minimize enchantment, as though Folen had been interrupted in his writing. Iddo often studied it, trying to figure out what had stilled his father's hand, trying to discover where and why and how his father had vanished without a trace.

Yasmin soon began to anticipate his visits, or so it seemed; she lifted her head when she heard his footsteps enter her underground home. (Some might call it a prison, but Iddo did not think it was so bad as that. There were walls, true, and chains, but she could move about freely in the spacious room. He had removed all his scientific tools, all his books, all the random items that could become something like a weapon in the hands of a monster. Sometimes he dearly missed the room, which had once been his experimental lab. But guilt made it quite clear that this was the price he had to pay for creating a monster like Yasmin.)

When Yasmin attempted some rudimentary magic—especially when she attempted it on him—Iddo realized that he could no longer allow her an education in magic. It was far too dangerous. No magic remained in him; he had passed his gift along to a son who had disappeared. Iddo was worth nothing in the fight against Yasmin, so he could not allow her to increase her magical abilities and potentially escape.

He did everything he could to ensure that Yasmin would remain inside the stone walls of his secret room.

And yet she had escaped. This he discovers when he brings a meal—the first one in three days—and notices that the last meal, in its entirety, remains beneath the small hole in the door through which only two arms and a plate can pass. Yasmin has never not eaten. She has a ravenous appetite. He knocks on the door. There is nothing.

He opens the door, peering into the darkness. She would use a light if she were here. In the beginning, he had given her an enchanted candle—one that never burned up. But the room is thoroughly dark. He shoves his torch into it, shadows licking at the corners.

With a quaking heart, he steps fully into the room, holding the blazing light before him as though it might protect him. The chains, he sees, are snapped in half. Yasmin is gone.

"Impossible," he says to no one but himself. "This cannot be."

She knows too much. She has too much power, acquired through education and some strange connection with the Grim Reaper. He should not have allowed her access to the books in his library.

He should never have let her read even a portion of the Old Man's Great Book.

Iddo turns round and round and round in the empty chamber, as though one of his revolutions might uncover the monster, hiding in a corner. But she is gone. She has escaped. And now the whole world is in danger.

He crouches to the chains and runs his fingers along their jagged edges. How had she managed it? Had someone helped her? If so, who?

Iddo rises, his dark brown robe swishing against his ankles as he crosses the room to the door. But before he can cross the threshold, the door slams shut. The lock clicks.

Iddo is stricken. He pounds on the door.

"Release me!" he says, his voice authoritative. "I am

Iddo, Prophet of Lincastle."

But whoever is on the other side of the door pays him no heed. He pounds again and again and again, until his fist is throbbing, but there is no answer from the other side of the door, except for the closing and locking of two more doors—his own security system turned against him.

The torch crackles in Iddo's hand. He stares at it, estimating how long he has until the light is gone. He must use his scientific mind. He must find a way out. After all, he is the one who created this room, this prison.

He sets to work.

The cart pulled by the bookseller of Lincastle, in which Oscar and Princess Freya are bound and blinded, rumbles along quickly, noisily, cutting through the Wishing Woods in record time. Princess Freya and Oscar cannot speak; they would not be heard above the din of the cart. But somewhere along their journey, her hand finds his, and they sleep off and on for what seems like hours. After all this time, Oscar will be delivered to the king of Fairendale. After everything Maude and Arthur had done to protect his life, after the Vanishing spell, after Princess Freya's kindness, it must end like this.

A hole opens in his chest, and his tears fall silently.

If only he could change things. If only he could find another way. If only he could rescue the princess and keep her safe, as he could not do for his little sister.

She wants to fly. Let her fly.

Oscar wishes with all his might.

And he feels it—feathers against his leg. Feathers against his hand. Feathers against his cheek.

He hears a flapping and a shout, and the cart suddenly pulls to a stop. His cape is ripped from his head, and the first place he looks is beside him. Princess Freya is not there. It cannot be. No. It cannot be.

But it is. There is a beautiful white swan, lifting into the air, then swooping through the air, then diving toward the bookseller and then back up, soaring toward Oscar, where it picks at the ropes and takes flight once more.

She lands in the cart, her white neck held in a graceful curve. "Princess Freya," he whispers.

The swan lowers her head, only for a moment, and then she beats her wings. The bookseller stumbles toward the cart.

"Where is the princess?" he says.

But Oscar can only laugh. The bookseller would not believe him. No one would believe him. He has turned the princess into a swan, simply by wishing.

The bookseller lunges toward the swan, but she is already too high. He curses and turns around, pointing a dirty finger in Oscar's face. "You will pay," he says. He stalks around to the front of the cart again and gives another cry—this one startled rather than angry.

"Tell me," says a voice, and Oscar's heart thumps. "What is it our friend has done to demand this rough treatment?"

The bookseller says nothing. Oscar struggles to his knees and peers around the horse. He expects, however unlikely it might be, to see Princess Freya standing before the cart, but it is not her. It is a woman, dressed in glittering green, with beautiful red hair waving in the wind. The woman locks eyes with him. He recognizes her as the woman who gave Maude and all the lost children of Fairendale a shoe-shaped house inside the Weeping Woods, and the knowledge sends a cold trickle down the back of his spine. Has she come to save him or take him?

The woman gestures toward the sky. He looks up and sees the white swan far above him. "And now she can fly," the woman says. "Some wishes do come true. How lovely."

It is this moment when Oscar realizes that he was not responsible for the transformation at all. It was the woman. The sorceress. She is the magical one.

Now that he can see, he analyzes his position and what he needs for a successful escape. And when he has fully analyzed it, he jumps to the ground, his hands still bound, and begins to run.

But he finds that he is running in place, stayed by an enchantment that restrains him somehow.

"Ah," the woman says. "You did not think you could escape me, did you?" He looks back over his shoulder, his legs still running but his position unchanging. "You are the first one for whom I have had to use a Restraint spell." She smiles, as though she enjoys this. "You will come with me, please." She touches her staff to the ground, and Oscar knows nothing more.

The Enchantress holds out her first finger, and, as though he is pulled by a force of nature rather than intellect, the boy turned into a blackbird dutifully flies to it. She places him in an iron cage and closes the door.

"Quite a collection now, I must say," the woman says. The bookseller backs away. She nods her head toward him. "And you." She does not say anything else, simply turns her staff slightly in his direction. He becomes a pigeon, the lowest of the pecking order in the village of

Lincastle. "There now. Someone else will have to run the bookshop, but I think you will find that wings are quite liberating." The pigeon flies off with a squawk.

The Enchantress turns to the Huntsman then, the bird cage lifted in her hands. "We have another," she says. "And now we must rest."

He catches her arm as she stumbles. He knows she is tired, but he must ask something else. "What about the princess?" he says.

"She is precisely where she needs to be," the Enchantress says. "The people cannot hurt a swan. They will never know she is a princess."

The words grab the Huntsman by the chest and shake him violently. She cares. He had not known she cared. And when her eyes meet his, the jolt becomes electrifying.

He is struck by the look in her eyes. It is an indiscernible look. Weariness, sorrow, triumph, all wrapped around one another. But this is not what strikes him most. No, the Huntsman is stricken by how green and beautiful the eyes of this Enchantress are. He remembers another girl with green eyes who once turned an old shoe into a bush of roses and cast him a glance that looked very much like this one while he sat in a back corner of his father's home and brooded about the loss of his best friend.

Oh, dear. It appears that the Huntsman's ruse is up. Have you guessed his secret, dear reader? He is not exactly who he calls himself (and, I must confess, there are several others like him in our story).

From here on out, perhaps we should simply call our Huntsman by his real name: Theo.

It is late evening. King Willis is in his throne room, pacing between the throne and the looking glass. He hears the castle doors burst open with a loud crack. He turns, startled, toward the throne room doors. Should he run? Should he attempt to hide in the secret passage in which he once found himself stuck tight? Should he remain?

He glances toward the looking glass. A click and then another sound outside the throne room doors. Someone is walking down the Great Hall. Someone is coming.

King Willis, though a thousand thoughts run through his mind—the loudest of which is: *Run*—remains, rooted to the spot. His legs do not obey what his mind tells them to do. This is one of the travesties that arise from a dark magic residing within a heart. The King Willis who, days ago, could think somewhat clearly and rationally, is still huddled in a shadowed corner of this shell-king's mind.

What was it his father had told him tonight, when he had reported on how the gathering of men is going? That he was a coward for not even having begun the work?

Well, perhaps it is true. Perhaps King Willis is a coward. In any case, he is powerless to move, and because of this he is standing still, facing the throne room doors. His eyesight, fortunately, is too poor to watch the brass knob turn ever so slowly—but it is turning.

Garth appears suddenly behind him, and the king nearly jumps right out of his skin when the boy speaks. "Your Majesty," Garth says.

King Willis tries to still his heart so as not to appear foolish in front of a servant.

"There is a…" Garth looks toward the throne room doors but seems unable to choose the next word. At last, he offers, "Creature."

"A creature?" King Willis says, and the cold dread freezes in his chest. His mind, though limited without the full possession of his former self, conjures up a great many creatures that could be creeping his way. "What kind of creature?"

"A creature…" the boy hesitates again.

"Well, go on," the king says, his voice rising more from fear than annoyance. The knob on the door continues to turn slowly. Garth glances toward it and back at his king.

"A creature here to see you," Garth says.

"How do you know it is here to see me?" King Willis says. "How do you know it does not come for you?"

"Because it told me," Garth says. And at that very moment, the throne room doors fling open, and there before the king is a bluish blur, with a bit of purple wrapped around it. The figure moves closer, and what slowly takes shape before the king is a creature that looks nothing like the ones his mind offered moments ago in a page-skim fashion.

King Willis squints his eyes. They have never been all that good at seeing what was far away. He always thought he needed spectacles, but he never mentioned it to his father; it would have been seen as yet another weakness.

The figure stops a few feet from him. "Your Majesty," it says in a low and harmonic voice that sounds nothing like the growl of a creature.

King Willis cannot find his tongue; he is still trying to make sense of this vision. He is quite certain the creature is a woman; she wears a purple dress that flows about her ankles. Her skin has a blue tint to it, just as he had thought. He stares at her, simultaneously trying to identify what kind of creature she is and also why she might be here, walking on two feet, visiting his castle.

She smells of earth and stone.

The creature moves a few steps closer. She bows. He can see her quite well now, and he sees that she has black stitches across her right cheek. She has more on her left arm and perhaps more where he cannot see it.

For a moment, the old King Willis returns to this shell of a body. It is, oddly, fear that brings him back and fear that then sends him just as quickly away. He would rather not know. The shell of King Willis remains, shaking.

"What business have you here?" King Willis says.

The creature lifts from her bow, which was graceful in a monstrous sort of way. Her eyes are large and black, but not so black as those creatures called Black Eyed Beings. When she smiles he sees that her teeth sit straight and white in her mouth. She is unlike any creature he has ever seen.

"My king," she says. "I have traveled long and far to help you."

"Help me?" King Willis says.

"I believe you will need my help," she says.

King Willis shakes his head, the fog in his mind gathering thicker clouds. "Why would I need your help?"

he says.

"Because I have at my beck and call all the creatures of the forest," the creature says. "And not just this forest, either. Every forest in the land. You would be surprised how few creatures it requires to build an army." She tilts her head slightly, and the king feels both revulsion and glee. Could it be so easy? Could an army be at his fingertips?

But what if she uses this army of creatures to turn against him? King Willis shudders. He does not even want to consider the implications of such a thought.

"Who are you?" he says.

"I am called Yasmin," she says. "It was not always so, but of late I have become the queen of the forest creatures." She smiles again. "The dangerous ones, of course."

King Willis stares at her for a long moment. He looks beside him, where Garth had stood moments ago, but the boy is no longer here. The king swallows a large and bulky lump in his throat, but it does nothing to lessen the fear with which he regards this creature. And after a moment of staring, the more primitive and panicked part of the king's brain wins. He flees, as fast as a man of his size can flee.

The sound of Yasmin's cackle chases him out the

door.

Yasmin, left alone in the king's throne room, considers the looking glass. She moves toward it, though she cannot say why. She stares into it, appraising her face, which is quite changed from what it once was, but not so monstrous as she had supposed. In fact, with her long, dark lashes and her wide eyes she might even be considered a beautiful creature. She runs her hand along the black threads that mark her right cheek. Her skin shifts a bit. She pulls her hand away. She will not be able to rid herself of the stitches, but it does not matter for what she has planned. She does not need to be beautiful.

She tilts her head and stares at her reflection. The black eyes stare back at her. She smiles. Her reflection smiles. And then it winks, though Yasmin herself has not done the same.

"Ah," Yasmin says. "Just as I supposed. A magic mirror."

She moves closer and touches the glass. Rings ripple from her finger, but she cannot breach its barrier. She stands back again. "Well," she says. "No matter. I will find a way. And then we shall have the kingdom we always deserved."

A smile spreads across the face of her reflection. Yasmin allows her own lips to stretch into the very same arrangement.

She crosses the stage and touches the golden throne. It emits a soft violet glow. She takes this as an invitation.

And she sits.

Queen Clarion, as usual, is consulting books in the castle library, paging through them to find any mention of a key that would unlock the dungeons beneath the dungeons. She has been reading all day. Her eyes grow weary. She rubs them, sits back in her wooden chair (she chose the most uncomfortable one to keep her awake), and stares at the ceiling for a time. She is just about to return to her reading when the library doors burst open.

Garth wears an ashen face.

"Someone is in the castle," he says before she can speak.

"Who?" she says.

"A creature," he says.

Queen Clarion jumps to her feet, fear dousing out her weariness like a sopping wet blanket beating a fire.

"Where?" she says.

"In the throne room."

Queen Clarion rushes out the door and down the great hall and into the doorway of the throne room. She does not enter, however. She senses that it would not be wise to do so.

But she does see. She sees a creature—half woman, half something else entirely—talking to a mirror.

The cold fingers of fear inch down her back.

Still in full possession of her wits, the queen turns and flies back to the castle library. She bolts the door behind her and pulls down every volume that might have some information about the mysterious creatures of the forests.

It will be another long night of reading for the queen.

When the children in the dungeons beneath the dungeons are only just drifting off to sleep, they are startled by the seemingly urgent voices of the three blind mice.

"We have news," Gus says.

"Quite bad news," Timmy says.

Florence shakes her head.

"What news?" Yerin says. He sits up and grasps the

iron bars.

"A creature has shown up at the castle," Gus says.

"She is not human," Timmy says. "But she is not fully creature, either."

Florence tilts her head.

"What is she, then?" Agnes says.

"Half woman, half creature," Gus says.

"Half…" Timmy says, but he cannot seem to think of another word.

Florence shakes her head again.

"I have never heard of such," Yerin says. "You are sure it is a creature and not a…" He searches his mind for what the visitor could be, but there is nothing.

"She is quite frightening to see," Gus says.

"Blue skin, black eyes, purple dress," Timmy says.

Florence holds up her walking stick, but Yerin and the children have no idea what she is trying to say.

"And where is she?" Yerin says.

"Sitting on the throne," Gus says.

"She is evil," Timmy says.

Florence grimaces.

Yerin grips the iron bars tighter. "And the king? Has she harmed the king?"

"No," Gus says. "She has come to help him. She calls herself the queen of the forest creatures."

"Yasmin," Timmy says.

"Yasmin?" Yerin says.

"That is what she calls herself," Gus says.

"It is the name she offered the king," Timmy says.

Florence nods.

"Though we can all invent names if we wish," Gus says.

"How do we know your name is Yerin?" Timmy says.

Yerin's neck grows increasingly warmer. "And where did she come from?" he says, glad, for once, that the light is so dim.

"She did not say," Gus says.

"Everywhere," Timmy says. "And nowhere."

Yerin's hands shake. He stares down at them, unable to explain the tremor. It is as though his limbs have a mind of their own. Their shake soon moves into his belly and his chest and even his throat.

"Perhaps it is someone who will help us escape," Agnes says. She has drawn even with Yerin at the bars, and her glassy eyes stare out into the nothingness. "Perhaps it is a good thing she is here."

Yerin begins to say something but decides it would be better to remain quiet. The girl does not need to lose her hope. The children and the prophets will be safe enough here.

But what of the king? His chest aches just thinking about the possibilities. He closes his eyes and tries to See the future, but the cloud is thick and gray over whatever Vision he might be given. He is nearing his One Last Great Act, and the magic will not permit him to See the many different outcomes. He must choose and allow the pieces to fall where they may. It is all any prophet has ever been able to do.

It is all Aleen did.

"Well," Yerin says. "Thank you for the news. Might we bother you for another of your stories?"

"Certainly," Gus says, and he climbs through the bars and arranges himself in a small tuft of white on the lap of Agnes. He begins, of course, with, "Once upon a time."

A story bends perfectly around those who await their freedom.

**Don't miss out on the next Fairendale
adventure!**

Find out what happens when the queen of dark creatures
discovers her power in Book 13: *The Woman Who Stole the
Throne.*

An Interview with Oscar

Transcribed by L.R. Patton
Author

L.R.: Tell me, what did you think the first moment you awoke in the kingdom of Lincastle?

Oscar: I thought, "Well that is disappointing."

L.R.: What was disappointing?

Oscar: I was still the same boy.

L.R.: You wanted to be someone different?

Oscar: Well, of course I wanted to be someone different. Did you see my boots?

L.R.: I did not have an opportunity to see your boots, I am sorry to say.

Oscar: You did not miss much.

L.R.: Those boots look quite nice, however.

Oscar: They are. I am exceedingly grateful to Princess Freya, who supplied them for me.

L.R.: She supplied a great many things for you. Tell me about your friendship with her.

Oscar: She was a lovely friend.

L.R.: Lovely, meaning…lovely?

Oscar: [red patches appearing on his cheeks] I mean she was good company to have around.

L.R.: But can you tell us why, specifically, she was good company to have around? I know our readers are curious.

Oscar: Because she likes to read and we could talk about books and she was kind and her eyes were the color of a Fairendale sky—

L.R.: So she *was* lovely.

Oscar: I do not want to answer any more questions.

L.R.: I am sorry, Oscar. I will not mention Princess Freya again.

Oscar: Lovely.

L.R.: She was lovely, was she not?

Oscar: We are done here.

L.R.: [laughing] I am sorry, Oscar. I must compose myself. I am not usually so…

Oscar: [scowling] Annoying?

L.R.: [shaking with laughter] Unprofessional.

Oscar: Is there anything else you would like to know, then?

L.R.: Yes. I am sorry. Yes, I would like to know more.

Oscar: Go on, then.

L.R.: [clearing throat] What do you think might have happened if the lovely Princess Freya—

Oscar: [standing up] It is time for me to go.

L.R.: But we have not even started the questioning.

Oscar: Well, you can only fault yourself.

L.R.: Please. Sit down.

Oscar: I do not think I am permitted.

L.R.: What do you mean you are not permitted? You

make your own decisions. You are a free boy.

Oscar: Perhaps I am not as free as you think.

L.R.: But we have so much more to cover. I have not even asked about why you think Princess Freya might have taken such an interest in you—

Oscar: Goodbye.

L.R.: Oscar?

Oscar: Until we meet again. [Under breath] Hopefully never.

L.R.: Oscar? Are you there?

Oscar:

L.R.: Oscar?

Oscar:

L.R.: Well, this is a most unsatisfactory ending to things. I did not even get to ask Oscar about his shelter and what it was like sleeping in an inn, which none of the other lost children of Fairendale have been fortunate enough to do. I suppose it *is* my own fault; next time I will tone down the teasing.

If you would like to read more Fairendale extras like this, be sure to visit www.lrpatton.com/fairendale.

5 Reasons Reading is Good for You

By Oscar
Lost Child of Fairendale

If you have read my story, you are well aware that reading got me into great trouble in the kingdom of Lincastle. Actually, it was not the reading itself, it was the action I took to enjoy the reading—but, in a way, it was the reading that called to me and thus told me I should do what I did.

My mother would like say I am blame-shifting, but books have always called to me; that is simply a fact.

Most of the time, my story excepted, reading is good for you. Actually, all the time it is good for you, provided you have a place where you can borrow books and do not have to steal. I believe your world has what is called libraries, where you can borrow all sorts of books to read. Use your libraries. I would.

Here are some reasons reading is good (use these on your parents if you would like to visit the library every day; they will not be able to resist taking you):

1. Reading provides you with information.

Do you know how many things I have learned from reading books? I cannot even quantify all I have learned. Books contain such valuable information. In my land, we can learn about every creature to avoid, why mermaid's

tails are good luck, the origin and intricate histories of all
the lands around Fairendale, what happens to the rain
when it soaks into the ground, why the sun rises the way
it does (though most people in Fairendale believe this
particular book was a book of fiction; my mother did not.
She believes every word of science that has ever been
written by a man called Iddo).

I am sure that in your land, you could read about all
sorts of things as well—former cultures and the people
who explored and settled your land (provided you read
the right accounts) and how to survive in the woods,
which you might need someday.

There are a great many things to learn, and reading
can bring that information to your fingertips.

2. Reading is entertaining.

If you are like me and most boys of Fairendale, you
hit a point in the afternoon when it feels as though you
have done everything you could possibly do to entertain
yourself—bugs no longer look interesting, woods no
longer need exploring (do not tell my mother I ever
explored them), tricks no longer need playing. Books
provide the perfect diversion from that oppressive feeling
of boredom that is likely to settle upon you at this point
in your day.

I like to read my books outdoors. I do hope the tree I
loved is still standing in Fairendale, slightly to the north
of the village, and did not get destroyed by the king's men

who marched through the streets the day I fled.

3. Reading introduces you to new words.

If you ever want to impress a parent or an instructor with new and interesting words, reading is the perfect opportunity to gather those words. Books contain so many words. I keep a bound journal of interesting words. Sometimes I ask my mother what they mean. She always points me to a very thick book called a dictionary. Would it be terrible to admit that I love reading the dictionary, too?

A larger vocabulary helps you express yourself—both in conversation and in writing—in more specific and clearer ways. Words, my mother says, are important. I believe her.

If you enjoy speaking and writing (and embellishing, I must say; the hole in my boot was not that bad. Well, yes it was.), you must add reading to your list of daily activities.

4. Reading introduces you to new worlds.

I bet you had never heard of Fairendale or even knew it existed before you read my story and the story of the other lost children. Are you not glad you picked up this book?

5. Reading develops empathy.

Empathy is an important characteristic to carry throughout your life. When we empathize, we step into the shoes of another person and examine how we would feel if we were them. Empathizing is important, because it helps you accept others for who they are and what they do, which leads to less misunderstanding and hate in the world. When we empathize, we can respond appropriately to any situation that comes before us.

Reading the stories of others helps us develop and exercise the power of empathy.

As you can see, reading has many benefits. When in doubt, pick up a book. You can always put it back down..though you likely will not want to.

5 Truths You Should Consider When Raising the Dead

By Iddo
Prophet and (Scientific) Healer of Lincastle

Death is a difficult reality to embrace when you are left behind. Trust me. I know. I lost my wife nearly four years ago, and my son ran away just after she died; I have never found him, though I have searched. I lost both of them, within days of one another. I have never recovered.

Loss has a hollowing out effect; it produces in you the kind of hole that feels everlasting. And perhaps it is.

This is precisely why some wish to raise the dead. They desire to bring back the ones they love because the ache of loss is far too painful, the longing far too pronounced.

Perhaps you already know that I am speaking of myself. My justification for what I have done is this: I am only human.

If I had been thinking with the logical part of my brain and not the deep well of sorrow, here are some things I might have considered before attempting—and failing with my wife but succeeding with Gladys, who became Yasmin—to bring someone back from the dead.

There is no guarantee that it will work.

It is only the most sophisticated of magic that can

bring a person back from the other side of death. Mermaids have this magic but use it sparingly. Mages are said to be the only sorcerers who have the ability. But science is always a wild card. Science can do a great many things; I thought it only logical that it could, with enough time and patience and hard work, raise the dead to life.

And it did, though the failures of my wife taught me many things, among them this: every attempt results in more decay for a dead body, which means attempts are limited. That is why, in the end, I let my wife rest and moved on to Gladys, or Yasmin.

You cannot predict what you will get when you raise a corpse to life.

When I thought of raising the dead, I envisioned in my head a body restored to whole life. I discovered, however, that once a body has been dead, it will never be the same body when raised to life. I did not consider this —for even a moment—in my quest.

It is unclear what makes a person rise from the dead —perhaps it is the reanimation of the brain, which is the control center of everything we know and perceive; perhaps it is the reanimation of the heart, which is the control center of our feelings and emotions. But it certainly is not the reanimation of the soul, which departs as soon as the body's breath is gone and likely goes somewhere we cannot see—to a better life after death, I would like to believe. What remains in the body after that shining soul is gone is only a small portion of light—and a large portion of dark.

Now that I have taken a step back from my studies, I can see how this would have been a logical conclusion at which to arrive; all I can say is that I simply was not thinking clearly.

Thinking with sorrow and desperation in attendance is a dangerous thing to do.

Reanimating a corpse could be dangerous.

As you have seen in this particular story, Yasmin was raised from the dead and became stronger and slightly larger and much more unstoppable than she was in her former life. I do not even know for sure that she will be able to die again, since she is the equivalent of the living dead; that would require testing I cannot do—not only because she is no longer in my work space, but also because I do not desire to perform these tests, since they would likely require attempts to destroy her.

If Yasmin is unstoppable, then you can see how this could be a dangerous thing: a reanimated corpse could do much damage in the world.

I hope she is not doing damage; I do not think the person she was would like to be a part of anything damaging.

Raising someone from the dead will not fill the hole.

The hole of death, the hole carved out by the ones we love so much, will not be filled by a portion of the person—what you get when you raise the dead. The hole remains, joined by others.

Life is not man's gift to bestow.

It is not a man's place to play the giver of life or death, and I should have known this. Had I stopped long enough to consider my actions, I likely would have concluded that I was overstepping my bounds as a former sorcerer, a man, and a scientist. We are not permitted the power to give life where it ceases to exist, and even if science is capable of it, ethical considerations say it is never worth the risks.

Do not make the same mistakes I have made in my life. Loss is a natural part of the life cycle, and it is much better to grieve and carry that hole of sorrow than to produce something that will not fill the hole but will, instead, gouge out other holes—holes of regret, shame, and inescapable fear.

I know you are wiser than I have been in my life.

How to Detect a Dragon in Camouflage

By Arthur of Fairendale
Former Teacher of Magical Studies

The whole of what I know about detecting dragons in their camouflage can be summed up in one sentence:

If they do not want you to see them, you will not.

You see Fire Mountains; they are actually dragons.

You see blades of grass, leaves on trees, shrubs and bushes; they are actually dragons.

There is no telling what else you might see that could actually be dragons.

The world is a fascinating place.

The Royal Family of Fairendale

King Willis: The current king of Fairendale. Son of King Sebastien. Has a deep love for sweet rolls.

Queen Clarion: The current queen of Fairendale. Is underestimated by her husband, but she will prove just how powerful she is in due time.

Prince Virgil: Son of King Willis and Queen Clarion, best friend of Theo. Prefers rye bread with melted butter to sweet rolls, depending on the day.

King Sebastien: Deceased king of Fairendale, exception to the line of boys who tried to steal thrones and were, upon failing at their quest, forever banished. Was killed by a blackbird.

The Former Royal Family of Fairendale

The Good King Brendon: Former king of Fairendale responsible for the alliance between the people of Fairendale and the dragons of Morad, lost the throne when it was stolen by King Sebastien. Killed in the Great Battle.

Queen Marion: Wife of the Good King Brendon, died mysteriously when her daughter was very young. Now lives in Lincastle and is "affectionately" called the

Evil Queen.

Princess Maren: Daughter of the Good King Brendon and Queen Marion. She has been missing since the Great Battle.

The Villagers of Fairendale

Arthur: Village furniture maker and magic instructor to girls who possess the gift of magic in the village of Fairendale. Is a bit reckless but always manages to come out on the other side—though one is not always assured it will be so.

Maude: Arthur's wife. Bakes spectacular pumpkin spice sugar cookies. Prefers caution to reckless abandon.

Hazel: Daughter of Arthur and Maude, twin of Theo. Cares for the village sheep and can even, amazingly, understand them. 12 years old.

Theo: Son of Arthur and Maude, twin of Hazel. Finishes his chores early so he can sit in on magic lessons. 12 years old.

Mercy: Daughter of Cora, best friend of Hazel. Prefers spectacular acts of magic to "boring" ones.

Cora: Mother of Mercy, widow, shape shifter. A woman who moves. Unofficial leader of the villagers in Fairendale.

Garron: The town gardener. Talks to plants as though they can hear him.

Bertie: The town baker. Enjoys showing off his air-kneading skills for the children. Or used to.

Staff of Fairendale Castle

Garth: Page for King Willis, the oldest of twelve children. No longer calls King Willis "Your Wideness" when he is feeling particularly prickly, because he knows how dishonoring it is to call names.

Cook: One of the few shape shifters in the land. Shape shifts into a bear. Is highly annoyed by her assistant, Calvin—but not really.

Calvin: An orphan who began working as Cook's assistant after his parents died in a Fire Mountain eruption in Ashvale. He is the only one allowed through the magical door to the dungeons beneath the dungeons and so is tasked with feeding the prisoners and keeping them alive.

Sir Greyson: Captain of the king's guard. Receives medicine, which keeps his mother alive, for his service to the king. Carries a magical sword that cannot be lifted by any but him.

Sir Merrick: Second in command to Sir Greyson.

Has a blind daughter named Agnes.

Gus, Timmy, Florence: Three blind, talking mice. Not technically staff of the castle, but they roam about it unseen, gathering information. It is suggested they were once people, transformed by a spell.

Important Prophets

Aleen: Prophetess who is one hundred forty-two years old, from the kingdom of White Wind. Wears ebony skin and what appears to be snakes for hair (though it is not). Sacrificed her life to change the fate of the Fairendale children in Book 6.

Yerin: Prophet who is one hundred forty-two years old, from the wild woodland between Lincastle and Eastermoor. Has white hair that makes the dark of the dungeons where he is imprisoned a bit less dark.

Folen: Former prophet of Lincastle, father of Iddo. Trapped in a looking glass created by Queen Marion. It was left on the grounds of Fairendale, just before the Great Battle.

Iddo: Prophet of Lincastle, son of Folen. Trained King Sebastien in both dark and light magic, though he is more scientist than sorcerer. Created a machine that can bring the dead to life again. It has only worked once.

Bregdon: Prophet of White Wind. Most powerful prophet in the land, known as the Old Man. Wrote and enchanted the Old Man's Great Book. Brought Queen Marion and the three Graces back to life. Has mysteriously disappeared.

Dragons of Morad

Zorag: King of the dragons of Morad. Wears green scales with an ivory belly. Lost his parents in the Great Battle, when King Sebastien stole the throne from the Good King Brendon. Would like nothing more than peace.

Blindell: Zorag's cousin, raised as the dragon king's son. Wears black scales and spikes all down his back. Lost his parents in the Great Battle, when King Sebastien stole the throne from the Good King Brendon. Would like nothing more than revenge.

Larus: One of the elder dragons of Morad, male. Counselor to Zorag. Wears blue-green scales that shimmer like water. Has a green horn on the top of his snout.

Malera: One of the elder dragons of Morad, female. Counselor to Zorag. Wears bright red scales and an ivory belly.

Alvah: One of the elder dragons of Morad, female. Counselor to Zorag. Ancient dragon who has been alive since before Zorag's father was born. Wears orange scales that used to be red but have faded in time.

Oned: One of the elder dragons of Morad, male. Counselor to Zorag. So ancient he is gray, colorless, with scales peeled off in places.

Kohar: Ancient food gatherer for the dragons of Morad, male. Wears pale yellow scales.

Other Important Dragons

Rezedron: King of the dragons of Eyre, uncle of Zorag. Dying of wounds sustained from a poisonous rose in Rosehaven, believed to be dark magic.

Residents of the Violet Sea

Arya: Twelfth daughter of King Tritanius, who rules the Violet Sea. Adventurous, impulsive, often considered rebellious by her father. Saves the Huntsman from death by fairy magic. Loves a mortal.

Other Important Characters

The Graces: Formerly mortal women who died and were brought back to eternal life by the Old Man. Now known as Splendor, Good Cheer, and Mirth, or, collectively, the Graces. Maintain the balance of good and evil in the realm. Cannot predict the future.

The Grim Reaper: Master of the dead. Leads an army of Black-Eyed Beings. Longs to be seen as something more than a passing shadow.

Yasmin: Frankenstein-like creature brought back to life by the scientific tools of Iddo. Formerly known as Gladys, mother of Sebastien, before he stole the throne of Fairendale.

The lost 12-year-old children of Fairendale

Ursula

Chester

Charles

Thumbelina (known as Lina among the children)

Minnie

Jasper: Transported to the land of White Wind by Hazel's Vanishing spell. Becomes a wolf who befriends a girl in a red cloak. Runs very fast.

Frederick

Ruby: Transported to the land of Rosehaven by Hazel's Vanishing spell. Becomes an old woman who meets Rapunzel, befriends her, and supplies her with chamomile. She is a masterful gardener.

Martin

Oscar: Transported to the land of Lincastle by Hazel's Vanishing spell. Remains exactly the same, even down to the holes in his boots. Loves to read, steals food by pretending to be a bird, and befriends a princess (he would never admit it is, more precisely, a crush).

Homer: Transported to the land of Rosehaven by Hazel's Vanishing spell. Becomes a dwarf who can spin straw into gold, otherwise known as Rumpelstiltskin.

Anna: Transported to the land of Eastermoor by Hazel's Vanishing spell. Becomes an old, bent woman who resides in the Were Woods. Is awkward with magic, which causes some unexpected problems.

Aurora

Rose

Edgar

Harriet (known as Hattie among the children)

Isabel (known as Izzy among the children)

Ralph

Dorothy

Julian

Tom Thumb

Philip: Transported to the forest outside Lincastle by Hazel's Vanishing spell. Becomes the leader of the Merry Men, otherwise known as Robin Hood. Can shoot an arrow straight to the target, even if the arrow is crooked.

Other lost children of Fairendale

August: One of the lost boys of Fairendale, escaped with Theo. Known as the leader of the lost boys. Resides in a rundown shelter in Lincastle. 11 years old.

Leopold: One of the lost boys of Fairendale, escaped with Theo. Resides with August and the other lost boys. 11 years old.

Fineas: One of the lost boys of Fairendale, escaped with Theo. Resides with August and the other lost boys. 11 years old.

Norman: One of the lost boys of Fairendale, escaped with Theo. Resides with August and the other lost boys. 10 years old.

Henry: One of the lost boys of Fairendale, escaped with Theo. Resides with August and the other lost boys. 10 years old.

Ernest: One of the lost boys of Fairendale, escaped with Theo. Resides with August and the other lost boys.

10 years old.

Agnes: Daughter of Sir Merrick, trapped in the dungeons beneath the dungeons of Fairendale castle. Blind, but quite good at hearing and sensing what others cannot.

About the Author

Though she has never been able to fly (nor has she tried), L.R. says that, metaphorically, we all have the opportunity to fly every single day. When first we wake to a brand new morning, she says, we have the opportunity to greet our world with kindness, humor, hope, and love —or we have the opportunity to stare at the ground and believe our day is already against us.

She prefers flying.

L.R. believes that flying also happens when we discover the dream locked inside all our hearts and we find the courage to chase it relentlessly. She does this every day, between the hours of 12:30 and 5:30 p.m., when she imagines worlds and people and stories with great, bursting joy that makes her feel as though she is flapping her wings and soaring. Pursuing a dream, she says, is a great way to fly.

When she is not repeating this to her children (who hate homework and love art, books, and computer programming), L.R. and her family fly together in other ways—visiting local museums, running on tracks (though she does not fly as fast as she used to), and playing kickball on their cement moat.

L.R. is the queen of her castle in San Antonio, Texas,

where she lives with her king and her six young princes,
who have, unlike **L.R.**, tried (multiple times) to literally fly
—unsuccessfully.

www.lrpatton.com

A Note From L.R.

Dear Reader,

I hope you have enjoyed this retelling of how Freya became a swan. The inspiration for this tale was borrowed from a not-so-well known Russian fairy tale called "The White Duck," upon which the more well known *Swan Lake* tale is based. I fused the two ideas—royalty turned into a bird, girl who becomes a swan—together and thought it would be worthwhile to examine why a person would turn a girl into a bird.

After reading this story, you might agree that there was good reason—Freya wanted to fly, and, more importantly, she *needed* to fly.

Sometimes it is not easy to see how something so fantastically undesirable—such as becoming a bird when one has only ever been a human—can be anything but problematic. It is not easy to see the twisting path as good. Time often helps straighten out the kinks, but perhaps it is enough to know that sometimes we need the wings that danger and darkness grant to us.

We can never really know how or when our wings will unfold. We can only embrace them when they do and use them every opportunity we get. Freya uses her wings to protect herself from the people in her kingdom. Cora uses her wings to question things. For what will you use your wings?

I use my wings to make sure children, youth, and adults feel seen, loved, and important.

Every book I write, regardless of whether it is part of the Fairendale series or it is some other imaginative tale, is written to

- Empower readers with hope, love, joy, peace, knowledge, and the necessary tools to make a better tomorrow
- Ensure that readers fall in love and stay in love with reading
- Foster in readers a love of language
- Encourage families to bond around meaningful stories
- Show readers characters who look like them
- Matter to the wider world.

I believe in the power of stories. I believe that stories have the power to inspire, inform, spread love, and effect real change in the lives of readers. And I write every book with this higher purpose in mind.

Though my writing is done alone, my world-changing is not. I need readers like you to help get my books into the hands of those who don't yet know the hope and inspiration that can be found in them. So here are some ways you can help:

1. Leave a review on Amazon.

Reviews help other readers find my books. The more readers who find my book, the better able I am to accomplish what I've listed above.

2. Tell your friends about this book.

Word of mouth is one of the most powerful tools we have for sharing the things we love—and it is, consequently, one of the most powerful tools I have for sharing my work with new readers.

I appreciate anything you can do to help my books get into the hands of readers and help create a literacy movement that matters.

My wings are growing restless, so I must return to my storytelling. In the future, please stop by my web site to say hello, to access some really fun bonus materials, or, perhaps, both.

In love,

L.R.

Acknowledgements

A book like this takes many, many drafts; many, many readers with helpful feedback; and many, many cheerleaders. The making and publishing of it would not have been possible without:

J—You wondered about a swan, and I wondered, too.

Ben—As always, I could never do what I do without you.

My launch team—Your loyalty is humbling.

Mom—Your encouragement is relentless. I'm exceedingly glad I get to call you Mom.

Thank you all for your presence, your life, your wonder and grace.

Enjoy more stories from the magical Fairendale series:

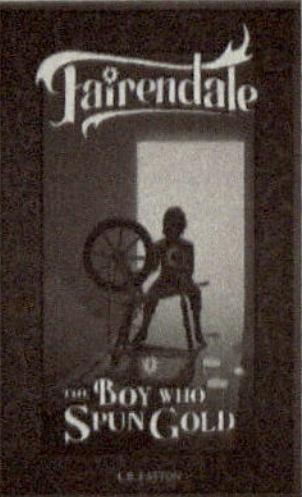

LRPatton.com/Fairendale

Starter Library

A singular obsession. A safe hiding space. A never-ending search.

The king's guard has been searching all the lands of the realm for the missing Fairendale children. But, alas, Captain Sir Greyson has returned, after many days, to report to King Willis that no children have been found. The king, quite angry at this disappointing news, orders another search, this one closer to home—right inside the dangerous Weeping Woods.

*Continue your journey into the world of Fairendale with Book 2: The King's Pursuit, a short story prequel, "The Good King's Fall" and some important bonus material, **free for a limited time.***

To get your FREE bonus materials, visit *
LRPatton.com/goodking

*Must be 13 or older to be eligible

www.ingramcontent.com/pod-product-compliance
Lightning Source LLC
Chambersburg PA
CBHW050613190726
48283CB00007B/2398